Prisoner of Dunes

By the same author

The Oblivion Seekers
In the Shadow of Islam

Isabelle Eberhardt

Prisoner of Dunes

Selected Writings

*Translated from the French
and with an Introduction by*
Sharon Bangert

Peter Owen · London & Chester Springs PA

PETER OWEN PUBLISHERS
73 Kenway Road London SW5 0RE
Peter Owen books are distributed in the USA by
Dufour Editions Inc. Chester Springs PA 19425-0007

'Blacks after Dark', 'Lost among Dunes', 'Homesickness' and
'Bled-El-Attar' first published by Editions Fasquelle, Paris.
The other selections in this volume were taken from *Écrits sur le sable*,
published by Editions Bernard Grasset, Paris, 1988
First published in Great Britain 1995
English translation and Introduction © Sharon Bangert 1995

All Rights Reserved.
No part of this publication may be reproduced in
any form or by any means without the written
permission of the publishers.

ISBN 0-7206-0944-5

A catalogue record for this book is available from
the British Library

Printed and made in Great Britain by Biddles of Guildford

Contents

Introduction	vii
Chronology	xiii
Market-day, Ain Sefra (*Autumn–Winter 1903*)	19
Blacks after Dark	23
Lost among Dunes	27
Bou-Saâda (*July 1902*)	43
Homesickness	51
Reminiscences	59
Memories of El Oued	63
Fantasia	65
Prisoner of Dunes (*El Oued, 18 January 1901*)	73
Marseilles, 16 May 1901	75
At the Military Hospital	79
El Oued, February 1901	83
Desert Springtime	87
Sojourn in Tunis	95

Amira (*September–October 1899*)	105
Bled-El-Attar	113
Marseilles, May 1901	123
Glossary of Arab Terms	125

Introduction

By the time I first heard of Isabelle Eberhardt, I had already begun collecting individuals, known to me mainly through books, who stirred me at such a depth that merely to read them was not enough; they urged me to further study, to work with their ideas, the example of their lives, in one way or another.

Peter Brook's film of G.I. Gurdjieff's *Meetings with Remarkable Men* set the standard for 'search' stories, for epic lives which have continued to pull me in their wake. Antoine de Saint-Exupéry's meditations on night flights and desert crashes pointed me towards the esotericism of *Le petit Prince*. Of Michel Vieuchange's fatal pilgrimage to the ruined *kasbah* of Smara in Morocco I was led to write a radio play. With Isabelle Eberhardt, I too was becoming a kind of 'prisoner of dunes' – just as willing a captive as she, in my imagined desert landscapes.

I located a copy of Eberhardt's *Dans l'ombre chaude de l'Islam*, irresistibly hooked by Cecily Mackworth's description of it in her Eberhardt biography as 'one of the strangest human documents that a woman has given the world'. My translation of that book was published in 1993, as *In the Shadow of Islam*, by Peter Owen.

I offer this background as a kind of credential. The reader should know that I am an enthusiast and an amateur, not a scholar or professional translator. And it is better that you know my inclinations, the zigzag path of my curiosity which has culminated, for the moment, in this book. My knowledge of French is not enough to deter me from translating; I lack the intimacy with that language which might otherwise cause me to throw up my hands at the futility, or injustice, of rendering into English what doesn't belong to it. Fools rush in here, as in love.

The chronology which follows gives the main events in Eberhardt's life. But the important things to know about her, which colour and determine those events, are that she was a Muslim, probably from some time shortly after she arrived in North Africa; and that she constantly dressed as an Arab man.

The easy rapport that seems to have existed between Isabelle Eberhardt and her male *alter ego*, Si Mahmoud Saadi, is to me one of the most fascinating aspects of the Eberhardt phenomenon. Imagine: you have put on the clothes and assumed the name of a man (not a Russian or Swiss such as you have lived amongst all your life, but an Arab man); you can speak Arabic fluently; and because of a peculiarly egalitarian upbringing in a family of brothers, you can hold your own in masculine company.

And yet Si Mahmoud, who was known variously as 'the little Turk escaped from a college in France', and 'the young Tunisian scholar', did not stand in the way of Eberhardt's womanly instincts. It is said that she had many male lovers, both French and Arab. We can be sure of one, Slimène Ehnni, the man she eventually married. Try to imagine the moment of revelation, the successive revelations, needed for such a love affair to begin. Then, while openly living with him in El Oued, she was initiated into the all-male, Kadriya Sufi sect of which Slimène was a member. What did her fellow Kadriyas read in the palimpsest Si Mahmoud presented to them?

She cannot have been fooling all the people all of the time. We allow for her achievement by invoking the Arab code of etiquette, which forbids questioning a person's own account of him or herself. As for the inconsistencies, as Eberhardt writes about the indeterminacy of the Algerian-Moroccan border: 'The present situation, hybrid and vague, agrees with the Arab character: it hurts no one and, so, should please everyone.' And yet, imagine Slimène arriving at Ténès to begin his new job. Meeting his colleagues, he introduced the slim figure in snowy *burnous* at his side as 'Si Mahmoud Saadi, Madame Ehnni'. The phenomenon is still hybrid, but no longer so vague.

I can accept that a masculine disguise was indispensable for Eberhardt's travels, for her integration into Arab and nomad life. What is marvellous was her daring to lift the mask, at crucial moments when trust allowed or desire dictated; her ability to be comfortable while knowing her disguise was transparent. We would be less shocked if she had behaved consistently, as a man in a man's world. If she had lived a careful, scrupulous, celibate life: the perfect man, the perfect Muslim, the perfect mystic – she would be tolerable. But she is maddening – to us, and therefore how much more so to her contemporaries, the French colonists, and to at least some of the native Arabs, like Abdallah ben Mohammed, who tried to kill her. The disguise we want her to wear is the one we all hide behind: the veil of predictability.

The selections in this book span the years of Eberhardt's North African sojourn, including the period of exile in Marseilles. They are not presented chronologically, though dates, when known, are given. Some pieces were titled, either by Eberhardt in her notebooks or upon subsequent publication; others bear only dates. The heart of the book consists of essays written from El Oued, or from Marseilles where she dreamed of El Oued. Reading them we realize that this 'town of a thousand domes' in south-eastern Algeria was itself at the heart of Eberhardt's North African adventure: it was the one place she dared to dream (briefly, vainly) of settling down; it was there she met the *spahi* Slimène, and became a Kadriya Sufi.

Eberhardt's writings about El Oued also express some of the most basic tensions that drove her. For El Oued appeared to Eberhardt as 'an enchanted city, as from the vanished centuries of earliest Islam'. It was both ephemeral and eternal, and therefore the perfect site of her heart's home, the Eden from which to be banished.

In the eponymous piece, 'Prisoner of Dunes', Eberhardt experiences ambivalent feelings about El Oued, a conflict between staying versus leaving. Struck by the reality of her isolation, she writes that 'the dunes disguise monstrous beasts that draw nearer... in order to enclose us more jealously, and for ever'. She contemplates leaving, both for reasons of health and because leaving would be an act of strength, of will, while her natural tendency is to stay.

However, events soon after transpired to relieve her of that choice. First Slimène, a military man, was transferred from El Oued to Batna, a move designed by his superiors to separate him from the already infamous Eberhardt. With Slimène gone, the tie that had bound her to El Oued was 'severed painfully', making her feel 'nothing but a stranger' there. Later that month, in nearby Behima, she was attacked by Abdallah, a man claiming divine inspiration for his deed; more likely a pawn, as Eberhardt was convinced, of his Tidjanya sect whose members were known enemies of the Kadriyas. Her account of the attack is given in her diaries, translated by Nina de Voogd in *The Passionate Nomad*. The selections in the present volume, taken from her notebooks, skip to her stay at the military hospital. From there she followed Slimène to Batna, only to be notified in May of her expulsion from French North Africa. Her brother lived in Marseilles, so she went there.

Newly arrived in Marseilles, she continued to write about El Oued and the Souf, echoing her earlier description of the dunes as monsters standing guard against her escape. But this version ('Marseilles, 16 May 1901') comes from an exile's perspective. The monstrous dunes are now invoked and rebuked for not guarding her and Slimène well enough.

In 'Homesickness' Eberhardt projects herself on to an anonymous 'he' whose 'soul was elect'. Of this persona she writes that 'during his far-off and successive exiles, [he] needed only an Arab-sounding word, an oriental melody, a perfume, even a simple bell ringing behind the wall of some barracks or other, to evoke with piercing clarity verging on pain a whole world of memories of the land of Africa, dormant, almost extinct, buried in the silent necropolis of his soul. . . .' This is the kind of remembering which Proust would later make famous and which Samuel Beckett, writing on Proust, would name 'involuntary memory'. Beckett, in his *Proust* essay (1931), goes on to describe a state of mind and an attitude which Eberhardt often exemplifies. Beckett writes that, during such experiences of 'involuntary memory', 'we are flooded by a new air and a new perfume (new precisely because already experienced), and we breathe the true air of Paradise, of the only Paradise that is not the dream of a madman, the Paradise that has been lost'.

Eberhardt relished nostalgia. One could almost say she was most at home in homesickness. With her first glimpse of a new land she anticipated her eventual departure, when the place would be transformed from merely real to an ideal.

Eberhardt tantalizes with what she leaves unsaid. We never learn how she coped with being Si Mahmoud/Isabelle/Madame Ehnni. Nor does she ever disclose the private world of the Kadriya mystics. But there is much to be read between her lines. For instance, how should we take her when, in the opening piece, she eulogizes the vagrant life: 'vagrancy is emancipation, and life on the roads is liberty'? It is a radical calling, to which few can or should respond, on a literal level. But the call is 'to arm oneself with the symbolic staff and bundle and *run away*!' By offering us the image of the tarot pack's Fool, with his staff and bundle, she signals our essential self to give heed.

In the book's final piece Eberhardt rises to the defence of suffering, calling it 'that beautiful, sublime and benevolent educator of souls'. Few in our secular age would have patience with this. We are in the habit of seeking out pleasure, not pain. Habit itself becomes our pleasure, like the drink we can order without a thought. But as Beckett, again in *Proust*, recognizes Habit as the defender of our vulgarity and the stifler of all true memory, so he values interruptions of Habit as 'perilous zones in the life of the individual, dangerous, precarious, painful, mysterious and fertile, when for a moment the boredom of living is replaced by the suffering of being'. None of us, however we may try, can avoid the perilous zones that intersect our comfortable, habitual lives. But a few, like Isabelle Eberhardt, actually cultivate them, and savour their fruits.

Arabic terms italicized in the text are defined in the Glossary at the end of the book. This and the Chronology were adapted and translated from the work of Eberhardt's most recent editors, Marie-Odile Delacour and Jean-René Huleu, in *Écrits sur le sable*.

This translation was completed at the Tyrone Guthrie Centre in Annaghmakerrig, Co. Monaghan, Eire. To all of its staff, particularly Bernard and Mary Loughlin, I am indebted for their deft and dedicated nurturing.

Sharon Bangert

Chronology

1872   Nathalie de Moerder, née Eberhardt, wife of the Russian General de Moerder, leaves St Petersburg to take up residence in Switzerland with her children's tutor, Alexander Trophimowsky. She brings her four children with her, and in Geneva gives birth to a fifth, Augustin.

1877   *17 February*: birth of Isabelle Eberhardt in Geneva. The identity of her father is not included on the birth certificate.

1894   Augustin de Moerder, Isabelle's half-brother, leaves Geneva to join the Foreign Legion of Sidi-Bel-Abbès.

1897   *From May*: Isabelle and her mother reside at Bône (Annaba) on the Algerian coast. *28 November*: death of Nathalie de Moerder, who is buried according to the Muslim rite in Bône. *December*: Isabelle returns to Geneva with Trophimowsky and stays there for a year and a half.

1898   In July Isabelle is engaged to marry Reshid Ahmed, a Turkish diplomat; but when he is posted to The Hague, she decides not to accompany him.

1899   *15 May*: Alexander Trophimowsky dies of throat cancer in Geneva. Isabelle leaves for Tunisia. *8 July*: she departs Tunis for the region south of Constantine. Her first experience of the Sahara and the town of El Oued, in the Souf. *2 September*: she returns to Tunis, travels in the Tunisian Sahel during September and October. *November*: visits Marseilles.

1900 *January*: travels to Sardinia. *February to July*: many trips between Paris and Geneva. *3 August*: arrival at El Oued, where she remains until the end of the year. Meets Slimène Ehnni, non-commissioned officer in the Spahis, a Muslim with French citizenship. Isabelle decides to share her life with him. She is initiated into the Kadriya brotherhood of Sufis and begins her friendship with the Kadriya chief, Sidi Lachmi ben Brahim.

1901 *January*: Slimène is transferred to Batna, because of his liaison with Isabelle. *29 January*: at Behima, near El Oued, a member of the Tidjanya brotherhood, Abdallah ben Mohammed, attacks Isabelle with a sabre, wounding her head and left arm. *25 February*: Leaves hospital at El Oued and departs for Batna, where she is put under police surveillance. *9 May*: believing herself to be under an expulsion order, she embarks at Bône for Marseilles. *18 June*: Abdallah's trial at Constantine, attended by Isabelle, who pleads for mercy on his behalf. He is sentenced to forced labour. Immediately following the verdict she is expelled from Algeria by the Governor-General. She returns to Marseilles to stay with her brother Augustin. *24 August*: Slimène is granted a transfer to another regiment. *28 August*: he joins Isabelle in Marseilles. *17 October*: they are married at Marseilles city hall.

1902 *15 January*: now French by virtue of her marriage, Isabelle is entitled to return to Algeria. A stay at Bône with Slimène's family; then the couple move to Algiers. *Spring*: Isabelle first meets Victor Barrucand. *June–July*: journey to Bou-Saâda and the El Hamel *zawiya*, where she meets Lella Zeyneb, holy woman and leader of the Rahmaniya brotherhood. *7 July*: move to Ténès, where Slimène is appointed *khodja*. Numerous trips between Ténès and Algiers. Barrucand revives the weekly newspaper *El Akhbar*, to which Isabelle becomes a regular contributor.

1903 *January*: second journey to Bou-Saâda and El Hamel; second meeting with Lella Zeyneb. *April–June*: Smear campaign directed against Isabelle and Slimène in connection with electoral politics in Ténès. Slimène resigns; is reassigned to Sétif. Isabelle moves to Algiers. *September*: she sets off for the 'Sud Oranais', the Algerian south-west, as a war reporter following the battles of El Moungar and the siege of Taghit. *October*: meets General Hubert Lyautey in Ain Sefra. She reports from Beni-Ounif on the situation along the Algerian–Moroccan border. Returns to Algiers at end of winter.

1904 Journey to Oujda (Morocco). *May*: second stay in the Sud-Oranais. Lyautey's troops occupy Bechar. Isabelle spends the summer at the Moroccan *zawiya* in Kenadsa. *September*: returns to Ain Sefra because of illness. *21 October*: Isabelle dies in a flash flood in Ain Sefra.

1907 *14 April*: death of Slimène Ehnni.

1920 Augustin de Moerder commits suicide in Marseilles.

One right to which few intellectuals care to lay claim is the right to wander, the right to vagrancy. And yet vagrancy is emancipation, and life on the roads is liberty: one day bravely to throw off the shackles with which modern life and the weakness of our heart encumber us, in a pretence of liberty; to arm oneself with the symbolic staff and bundle and *run away*!

For whoever values the delights of solitary freedom (and true freedom depends on solitude), the act of running away is most courageous and most beautiful.

Selfish happiness, perhaps. But happiness indeed for those able to appreciate it.

To be alone, to be *poor in needs*, to be unknown, a stranger and at home everywhere, and to march tall and solitary towards one's conquest of the world.

The committed tramp, seated at the roadside, contemplating the horizon's welcoming breadth – is he not absolute master of lands, waters, and even of heaven itself?

What landowner can rival him in power and riches?

His freehold has no boundaries, and his empire no laws. No servitude makes him shuffle, no labour bends his spine towards earth, which he possesses and which bestows on him the fullness of her bounty and her beauty.

In our modern society the nomad, the vagabond 'without domicile or known residence', is a pariah. By appending those few words to the name of some misfit or other, men of law and order believe they can blight him for ever.

To have a domicile, a family, a property or public function, definite means of existence, to be in the end an accountable cog in the social machine – such things seem necessary, almost indispensable to the huge majority of men, even to intellectuals, even to those who believe themselves most free.

They are all, however, various forms of slavery, compelling us into contact with our fellows, a contact mainly regulated and predictable.

I have always listened with admiration, but without envy, to the accounts of good folk who have lived twenty and thirty years in the same vicinity, indeed in the same house, who have never left their home town.

Never to have felt the torturing need to know and to see what's out there, beyond the mysterious blue wall of the horizon; never to have felt depressing suffocation in the same old setting; to see the road leading away in all its whiteness towards unknown distances without hearing the command to give oneself to it, to follow it obediently, across mountains and valleys – all this fearful need for immobility resembles the unconscious resignation of the beast stupefied by servitude, offering its neck to the yoke.

To all ownership, there are limits. Every force is governed by laws. But the vagabond possesses the entire vast earth, bounded only by the imaginary horizon. And his empire is intangible, a realm of spirit where he has his enjoyment and dominion.

Market-day, Ain Sefra

Since Sunday evening, on all the tracks, across all the dunes, nomads arrive on horseback, muleback, by foot, driving patient little donkeys and large, slow camels whose supple necks and greedy lower lips stretch towards tufts of green *alfa*. Ever-migrating tribes like 'Amour' and 'Beni-Guil' set off for Ain Sefra and its big Monday market.

The market plays a prime role in the life of Arabs, particularly Arab nomads. It's the place for meetings and reunions, for picking up the news, and for earning a little money.

From daybreak, on a vacant site between the village and the cavalry quarters, the crowd gathers, creating a din that will keep increasing till noon. Camels groaningly kneel; horses, tethered to the boulevard's slender acacias, snort and whinny to the passing mares. Men rush about, yelling.

Over all this uproar rise the plaintive bleatings of countless sheep tied together by the neck, and the bellowings of diminutive black bulls and cows. On the ground, merchandise from the south accumulates in magnificent disorder: fleeces stinking of grease; unrefined salt in spongy grey hunks; goatskins full of sour milk, butter or thuya gum; baskets woven of *alfa*; blankets and *haiks* in bright colours; stiff new *burnouses*; horseshoes; earthenware jars; skeins of wool yarn; saddles, and more.

And amongst this charming chaos of objects for sale, the nomads circulate: 'Amour' tattered and proud; 'Beni-Guil' in earth-coloured rags girdled with leather cartridge belts.

The women also mingle in groups, most often old ones, wasted, desiccated, with tattooed faces tanned by long summers, their bearing assured and their gestures masculine. More rarely one sees a younger face, with beautiful blue eyes and white teeth, half hidden under a long embroidered veil.

Since the Beni-Guil have obtained the *Aman* and begun earning profits from the frontier, they have a new lease on life after the dreadful misery they underwent last year during several months when they occupied the mountain. These highwaymen have retracted their claws. They circulate in the village, already less tattered if not less wild than before. They pass by, regarding us northern and eastern renegades with indifference, almost with disdain. They finally make up their minds to enter the shops; but mistrustfully, they stick together. There, interminable hagglings begin. The nomads debate for hours, consulting over trivial purchases.

In the Moorish cafés, they come together in threes or fours to take a little tea with a piece of dry bread. What heads they have, surmounted by wide turbans swathed in veils! What predatory profiles, with their flashing eyes and noses curved like rapacious beaks.

At the market, arguments break out over the slightest disagreement. From the sound of their voices, you'd think you were in the Moroccan no man's land, far from all supervision. For out there, in the even more tumultuous markets, gunpowder talks, corpses roll amongst the goods, blood flows over the beaten earth. Here, the Beni-Guil content themselves with extravagant gestures, threats and heroic insults:

'Just wait, infidel, bastard! We've got soft here, we've become like women from eating white bread and drinking running water. But wait till we get beyond Fortassa and have been drinking rainwater out of puddles! Then you'll see what we're made of!'

Against the red background of the soil, neutral shades stand out – ochre clothing, dull rust and beige of the camels, glossy black cattle and goats, the rose-tinted grizzle of sheep's crowded backs.

Such a harsh tableau – violent, yet full of life – of nomadic ways unchanged, untouched by the sweep of centuries.

Autumn–Winter 1903

Blacks after Dark

Occasional cries spill from the village canteens: hell-raising legionnaires arguing and singing. Here, in the 'black village', those sounds die away. The full moon spills a stream of blue light on to the grey brick houses, the empty streets, and on to the nearby dune, making it seem translucent.

From a little Moorish café, whose door is still ajar, a ray of red light glides over the sand, up to the opposite wall. Wild sounds, of tom-tom and singing, escape from this whitewashed hovel. We enter, the negro Saadoun and I.

You have to cross a room no bigger than a cell, then penetrate to the courtyard through a barely passable hole. Amongst the rubbish, in the diffuse light from above, a group of women are in restless motion.

Two old ones, squatting in the shadow, beat a drum and sing in their incomprehensible dialect, a long-drawn-out chant broken by a kind of savage panting, a rough, staccato rattling from the throat.

Three other negresses dance. One of them is young and beautiful. Her long, supple body bends, undulates and leans back slowly, shimmying, while her round, firm arms describe a passionate embrace. Then her head rolls on her shoulders and her wide russet eyes narrow while a languorous smile parts her lips, revealing flawless teeth.

Silvered reflections flow over the stiff silk pleats of her long, sky-blue tunic. The stuff floats around her shoulders like great airy wings. Her heavy silver jewellery marks the beat; whenever she claps her hands her bracelets clank like chains.

Her two partners, women with faded faces, mummies' masks, shake blood-red veils over their sluggish bodies. Opposite them, seated along the wall, the men watch the prostitutes' dance, a rite carried over from the Sudanese homeland, which takes place with every full moon.

There are four or five negroes, two of whom are pure Sudanese, examples of rare and deceptive negro beauty: fine features, long dark eyes, completely Arab. Their cheeks are adorned with branded scars and a silver ring pierces the lobe of their right ears. Unmoving, expressionless, transfixed by the dance, they watch in silence. The others, Kharatines and half-castes, laughingly grimace and point like apes.

Only one white among them, a *spahi*: with a fine Arab face from the highlands, he is the beautiful negress's lover. Leaning on his folded red *burnous*, he watches, too, in silence. A deep furrow gathers his arched eyebrows, narrowing the gleam of his black eyes that flash with his changing emotions. Sometimes, when the dancer swoons, her eyes smiling at him, the *spahi*'s entire body seems to reach ... then, when her attention turns to the laughter and jesting of the blacks, the nomad's restless hands, smooth and pampered, clench convulsively.

He doesn't even notice us enter. All his soul is devoted to contemplation of the woman who has made him forget his hearth-fire, his children, his friends, who has possessed him and keeps him there, in her dilapidated hovel.

In a small adjoining room a burning candle is stuck in

a bare white niche in the wall. A dozen negroes are half reclining on mats, and on colourful robes. Within reach, a copper platter holds glasses of tea and small *kif* pipes. White rags cover their black, sinewy bodies; dirty muslin veils prognathous, thick-lipped faces; here and there a scarlet *chechiya*.

The two Sudanese from the courtyard have followed us in. They sit side by side at the back of the room. One of them takes up a *bendir*, and the other a pan-pipe.

Then one of the negresses brings a clay incense burner with some benzoin and cinnamon bark smouldering over hot coals. The wisp of blue smoke slithers along the vaulted ceiling, soon filling the nook and thickening the air with its heavy warmth.

The two blacks begin their music, slowly at first, almost lazily. Then, little by little, they work themselves up. Drops of sweat bead on their brows, the dark pupils of their eyes dilate and their nostrils flare. They lean backwards, rolling around on the mat like drunks.

The man with the *bendir* raises his instrument at arm's length above his head and strikes, strikes with muffled beats, steadily accelerating to a mad rhythm. The piper, his eyes closed, sways his turbaned head.

The others sing without stopping, almost without breathing, the same panting song, the terrible song which, outside, stirred up the negresses' sweaty flesh.

The *kif* pipes make their rounds.

Gradually the mint tea, incense, music, and their own reek pervading the stuffiness of the room, combine to inflame the negroes' streaming brows. They convulse in a kind of madness.

Suddenly the handsome Sudanese playing the drum furiously throws it on to the incense burner. The thin skin of the *bendir* breaks, causing a burst of laughter. In a rage, the negroes tear the instrument apart.

And the pipes keep weeping a lament to the infinite, a melody of heart-rending sadness. I get out, my head of fire.

In the courtyard, the women have lit a fire of dry palm leaves. Its harsh brilliance exaggerates their wanton contortions.

Reclining on his red *burnous*, the *spahi* contemplates his mistress who grows more loose-limbed and excited with the passing hours. He hasn't budged, but the crease between his eyebrows has deepened.

I imagine how the night will end here in this black slum, where smouldering sensuality is fanned into flames of arousal. Outside all is quiet, everything dreams and rests in the cold light of the moon. It's a relief to gallop away in the fresh breeze of midnight upon the deserted road, to flee the dark intoxication of that terrible black orgy.

Lost among Dunes

At the end of autumn 1900, nearly into winter, I was camping with a few shepherds of the Rebaia tribe in a desolate region south of Taibeth-Gueblia, on the road from El Oued to Ouargla. We had a sizeable herd of goats as well as a few wretched camels: thin, worn-out strays from the In-Salah expedition by which the Saharan camel population had been decimated over the years, since most never returned from their distant convoys to El-Golea and Igli.

There were eight of us, including my servant Ali and myself. We were living under a large, low tent of goatskin which we'd set up in a slight depression between dunes. The first scant rains of November had coaxed forth the Sahara's strange plant life. We passed our days hunting the countless desert hares, and mostly day-dreaming, gazing out at the rolling horizon.

The calm and monotony of this existence, though never boring, brought forth in me a very gentle sort of mental and moral negligence, a salubrious relaxation. My companions were simple, rough men – though not at all coarse – who respected my dreaminess and my silences. They were very quiet themselves, for that matter. The days flowed by, peacefully, calmly, without adventure or incident.

Then one night as we slept in our tent, each rolled in his *burnous*, a violent south wind came up and soon blew into a storm, raising waves of sand. The bleating flock cleverly managed to huddle so close to the tent that we could hear the goats' breathing. There were even a few that came right into our shelter, and with the roguishness of their kind, stayed put there despite our presence.

The night was cold, so when a kid insisted on burrowing under my *burnous* and lying against my chest, and responded to all my attempts to expel him with stubborn butts of his head, I grudgingly welcomed him.

Tired after a full day of wandering, we soon fell asleep again despite the wind's ominous roar through the maze of dunes, and the incessant spray of sand, so like the sea, raining on to our tent. Suddenly we reawakened with a start and in confusion – flattened, smothered, under a very heavy weight: a violent squall had toppled our tent and brought it down on our heads. We got out by creeping on our bellies, with great difficulty, into the black night, where the cold wind was raising a furore under an inky sky.

Impossible either to erect the tent in the darkness or to light our little lantern. It must have been three o'clock by this time, and we preferred, crossly, to bed down under the stars and wait for day. Ali still had to extract, with much trouble, some blankets and *burnouses* from beneath the tent, as well as rescue the leaping, panicky goats.

I was suffocating in my *burnous*, upon which the sand continued to rain down; and what with the frightened bleatings, and the kicks of my poor horse, tethered to a stake, who was being jostled by the worried goats, I didn't manage to get another wink of sleep.

The wind died with startling suddenness. Ali got busy

lighting a large fire of brushwood. We all sat around the comforting blaze, chilled and stiff. Only Ali maintained his habitual good humour, poking fun at the rest of us – the exhumed, the undead.

The day broke limpid and calm over the desert, where the night's fury had etched a pattern of faint grey furrows in the sand, like the storm's fingerprints. I took a notion to go for a gallop across the plain which stretched beyond the belt of dunes enclosing our depression. Ali stayed behind to raise the tent and restore order to our equipment which had been scattered and inundated with sand. As I set off, he cautioned me not to roam too far from camp.

But as soon as I reached the plain I gave rein to my faithful 'Souf', who took off at full speed, as much in need as myself of dispelling the night's misery. For a long while we ran with abandon, drunk on space, in the serene calm of dawn.

Finally managing to slow Souf to a walk, I turned her round and saw we were already quite far from the dunes. Not wishing to return to camp too soon, I had the idea of going by way of the hills surrounding the plain. Soon I was entangled in a maze of hillocks, rising higher and higher, while setting a course towards the west.

There were valleys there similar to ours where I let Souf trot so as not to lose too much time. Little by little clouds gathered again, bringing a wind, but such a weak one that it would have had no effect at all on the surface of the ground, except that the night's gusts had stirred up and dried all the superficial layer of sand. So it was as if the earth had been pulverized, with sand continuing to flow gently from the steep dunes. I soon saw that my tracks were quickly disappearing.

After an hour I began to be amazed that I hadn't yet arrived at camp. It was getting late, and the heat was becoming oppressive. However, I was surely still climbing towards the west...?

Finally I halted, admitting to myself that I must have taken the wrong direction and gone past the camp. But I was still perplexed. Which way should I go? I had no way of knowing if I was above or below the correct route; that is, whether I had passed to the north or to the south of our camp. Finally I decided to head unswervingly northward, the less dangerous direction in any case.

But there again after an hour's ride, I came upon nothing, and so headed back towards the south. It was three o'clock in the afternoon now, and I was not amused at my predicament. All I had was a loaf of Arab bread in the hood of my *burnous* and a bottle of cold coffee. I started to wonder what would become of me if I didn't find my way before nightfall.

Leaving Souf in a valley, I climbed up the highest dune in the area. Around me on all sides I saw nothing but the grey surge of sandy hills, and I couldn't begin to understand how I had managed in so little time to lose myself so completely.

Then, wanting to avoid any more useless wandering, fearing to be overtaken by night in some barren place where my horse, already thirsty, would not even find any grass, I began searching for a comfortable valley where we could pass the night. Tomorrow at dawn, I thought, I'll set off towards the north until I reach the Taibeth road....

I discovered a long, deep vale where a leafier sort of vegetation was growing, extraordinarily green. I took the saddle and bridle off Souf and left her there while I played Robinson Crusoe. In the middle of an open area I found a pile of cinders only slightly mixed with sand, and a few hare bones: hunters must have passed the night there. Perhaps they would return?

Saharan hunters are rough, primitive men living under

the open sky, always on the move. Some of them leave their families far away, in the *ksour*; others are true men of the sands, wandering with wives and children. But they are the rare few, who live a life as free and uncomplicated as that of desert gazelles.

Among these hunters, there are quite a few 'irregulars', in solitary flight from the law of man. However, in these regions where towns and villages are relatively frequent, the 'dissidents' as they're called in administrative jargon, are seldom encountered. So I was hoping for the reappearance of last night's hunters as a means to escape my ridiculous situation. How worried my companions must be, especially the loyal Ali.

An excited whinny tore me from these thoughts: Souf had approached an especially lush, green thicket and was thrusting her head into the branches. She had discovered the unexpected – a *hassi*, one of the numerous Saharan wells often lost beyond the range of the regular routes; narrow, deep shafts known only to desert guides. It was the presence of this water at not too great a depth that explained the relatively dense vegetation in this valley. I tied my bottle to the end of my belt and lowered it into the well. Suddenly, just behind me, a voice spoke:

'You there. What are you doing?'

I turned. Before me stood three dark-skinned men, almost black, in ragged clothing, carrying their meagre baggage in cloth sacks and armed with long flintlock pistols.

'I'm thirsty.'

'Are you lost?'

'I'm camping not far from here with some Rebaia and some Souafa shepherds...'

'Are you a Muslim?'

'Yes, thanks be to God.'

The one speaking to me was almost an old man. His hand reached out to touch my chaplet. 'You are from

Sidi Abd-el-Kader Djilani... so we're brothers. We, too, are Kadriya.'

'God be praised,' I said.

My joy was intense at finding these nomads to be Sufi brethren. Fellow initiates of the same sect are bound by a rule of mutual aid and solidarity. They, too, were wearing Kadriya chaplets.

'Wait; we have a rope and a can. We'll water your horse and you can pass the night with us. Tomorrow morning we will lead you back. You've wandered too far south past the Rebaia camp. Now, even taking short cuts, it's at least three hours away.'

The youngest of them began to laugh: 'You've certainly brightened up!'

'What tribe are you?'

'My brother and I are from the Ouled-Seih, at Taibeth-Gueblia. And Ahmed Bou-Djema here is Chaambi from around Berressof. His father had a garden at El-Oued, in the Chaamba colony centred in the village of El Akbab. He left, though, the poor fellow...'

'Why?'

'Because of taxes. He set off for In-Salah with our *cheikh*, Sidi Mohammed Taieb. When he returned, he found his wife dead from typhus and his garden robbed of all its crops. So he took to the desert – all because of taxes.'

While this young Seihi was talking, my attention had been drawn to his primitive features and the cunning look in his big tawny eyes. He was a perfect example of the nomad race, strongly cross-bred with the oriental Arab, a mixture most characteristic of the Saharan peoples.

Ahmed Bou-Djema, thin and graceful, seemed to be older, as far as I could tell, since half his face was veiled in black in the Tuareg fashion. Whatever his age, his beautiful head was that of an old trail-blazer, aquiline and sullen. Hanging from his belt were two fine-looking hares. He moved off a few paces from the well, said *'Bismillah!'* and began to clean his game.

* * *

The sun had disappeared behind the dunes, and the last pink rays of light lay upon the earth between the sharp-leaved bushes and the jujube trees. The tufts of *drinn* seemed golden in the great red glow of evening.

Selem, elder of the two brothers, drew apart from our group, and spreading his ragged *burnous* on the sand he began to pray gravely, as if exalted.

'You have no family?' I asked Hama Srir, while we dug a hole in the sand in which to cook the hares.

'Selem has his wife and children at Taibeth. My wife is at the Remirma oasis, on the Oued Rir, at the home of her aunt.'

'Don't you worry, so far from your family?'

'Our fate is in the hands of God. Soon I'll go and visit my wife. When Selem's children are grown, they will hunt like their father.'

'In sh'Allah!'

'Amine.'

I was completely charmed and attracted by the free and careless life of these sons of the magnificent, mournful Sahara. After having rolled and tied the hares we placed them, still in their fur, at the bottom of the hole under a thin layer of sand. Then on top we lit a brushwood fire.

'So, were you married among the Rouara?' I asked.

Hama Srir made a vague gesture. 'That's a long story! You know that we Arab nomads hardly ever marry outside of our tribe....'

These hints piqued my curiosity. If only Hama Srir could be persuaded to tell me the story, which I imagined would be simple, yet stamped with the melancholy charm of everything having to do with the desert.

After our meal, Selem and Bou-Djema went straight to sleep. Hama Srir, reclining near me, took out his small string bag containing *kif*. I too carried in the pocket of my *gandoura* these emblems of a true Sufi. We began to smoke.

'Hama, will you tell me your story?'

'Why? Why are you interested in the affairs of people you don't know?'

'I adopt you as my brother, as a fellow Kadriya.'

'Brother,' he said, pressing my hand, 'what's your name?'

'Mahmoud ben Abdallah Saadi.'

'Listen, Mahmoud, if I too didn't adopt you as a brother, if we were not already brothers because of our *cheikh* and our chaplet, and if I didn't see that you are a *taleb*, I would be very angry about what you ask, for it's not the custom to talk about one's family. But listen, and you will see how God's decrees are all-powerful, and that nothing can deflect His will.'

* * *

Two years earlier, Hama Srir was hunting with Selem in the region of the fortress of Stah-el-Hamraia, near the great salt plains along the route from Biskra to El Oued. It was summer. One morning, Hama Srir was bitten by a horned adder and ran to the fortress: the keeper's old mother-in-law, a woman of the Rir region, knew how to cure all illnesses – at least those God permitted to be cured.

The keeper had left for El Oued with his son, and the fortress was left in the care of old Mansoura and her middle-aged daughter, Tebberr. Towards evening, Hama Srir felt much better and left the fortress, to rejoin his brother in the Bou-Djeloud plain. But, still slightly feverish and thirsty, he went first to the fountain situated at the base of the reddish, bare hill of Stah-el-Hamraia.

There he found Saadia, the eldest of the keeper's

daughters. She was thirteen years old and already a beautiful woman in her tattered blue robes. And Saadia smiled at the nomad, fixing him with a long look from her large brown eyes.

'In fifteen days I shall return to ask your father for you,' he said.

She shook her head, saying, 'He'll never allow it. You are too poor. You're a hunter.'

'I shall have you anyway, if it's God's will. Now go back to the fortress and keep yourself for Hama Srir, for whom you are promised by God.'

'*Amine!*'

And slowly, bent under her heavy goatskin full of water, she set off on the steep path towards the solitary fortress.

Hama Srir said nothing to Selem about his encounter, but he grew dreamy. 'It's not a good idea to talk about love and such things. It brings bad luck,' he explained.

Every evening when the sun kissed the blood-red desert and declined towards the salty Rir, Saadia went down to the fountain to wait for 'him to whom God had promised her'.

One day when she was out in the burning noon hour tending her herd of goats, she thought she would faint: a man, dressed in a long *gandoura* and white *burnous*, armed with a long flintlock gun, climbed towards the fortress.

Hastily she hid herself in the corner of the courtyard where she had her humble dwelling and, trembling, she whispered an invocation to Djilani, 'the Emir of saints', who was her patron.

The man entered the courtyard and called out to the old keeper: 'Abdallah ben Hadj Saad, my father is a hunter who belongs to the tribe of Ouled-Seih, from the town of Taibeth-Gueblia. I am a healthy man with a clear conscience, as God is my witness. I come to ask permission to enter your house. I come to ask you for your daughter.'

The old man frowned. 'Where have you seen her?'

'I haven't seen her. The old women in El Oued told me about her.... Such is destiny.'

'By the supreme word of the Koran – as long as I live, no vagabond will ever have my daughter!'

Hama Srir looked long at the old man. 'Don't swear about things you know nothing about. Don't play with the hawk – he flies through the clouds and looks straight at the sun. God will have His way, no matter what we do.'

'I have sworn.'

'God will judge,' said Hama Srir. And without another word he went away.

Si Abdallah, indignant, turned back into the house, and said to his daughters Saadia and Emborka, 'Which of you two little bitches let that vagabond see your face?'

Both girls kept silent.

'Si Abdallah,' their grandmother answered for them, 'that man came last month to have a snake-bite dressed. Tebberr helped me, as she's old now anyway. The man didn't see either of her daughters. Tebberr and I are old women, not worth hiding away. We cared for the wounded nomad according to God's law.'

'Watch them, so they don't go out.'

Saadia, her heart grieving, continued however to wait steadfastly for Hama Srir's return. For she knew that, as God had destined them for one another, no one could keep them apart. She loved Hama Srir and was confident.

* * *

Almost a month went by since the hunter had climbed to the fortress to ask for Saadia, without his reappearance. He was not far away, though, but was lingering in the *chotts*; and every night the ferocious hounds of Stah-el-Hamraia would bay.

He, too, had sworn.

One evening, his wife being ill, Si Abdallah relaxed his fierce surveillance, and ordered Saadia to go down to the fountain, but not to tarry. It was already late, and the young girl went down, her heart leaping.

The full moon rose above the desert, bathing it in blue light. The dogs made a furious racket in the otherwise silent night.

While she filled her *guerba*, her arms in the basin's water, Saadia saw a shadow pass between the fig trees in the garden.

'Saadia!'

'Praise God!'

Hama Srir seized her by the wrist and carried her off.

'I'm afraid! I'm afraid!'

She placed her trembling hand in his strong one and they set off running towards the Bou-Djeloud plain, in the direction of the Rir. And when she cried 'I'm afraid. Please stop!' he lifted her firmly in his arms and kept running, for he knew that this hour was his and that all the odds were against him. They fled and the baying of the hounds lost its frenzy.

* * *

The old man, surprised and annoyed by his daughter's prolonged absence, left the fortress and called out to her repeatedly. But his voice fell flat and unanswered in the heavy silence of the night. A shiver passed through his limbs. He hurried back in for his gun and went down to the fountain.

The can was floating on the water and the empty *guerba* was lying on the ground.

'Bitch! She's run off with that vagabond. The curse of God be on them!' And he turned back in anger, without a tear or a moan.

'Whoever sires a girl ought to strangle her at birth, to keep shame from invading his house,' he said, returning home. 'Wife, you have only one daughter now – and that one is too many! You've never known how to control them.'

The two women and Emborka began to weep and lament as over a corpse, but Si Abdallah made them shut up.

* * *

Meanwhile the two lovers had fled a long while across the sterile plain.

'Please stop,' begged Saadia. 'My heart is strong but my legs are worn out. My father is old and proud. He won't follow us.'

They sat on the salty earth and Hama Srir began to reflect. He had kept his word; Saadia was his, but for how long? He finally resolved, in order to frustrate any pursuers, to lead her to Taibeth and there to wed her before the *djemaa* of his tribe, without a marriage certificate.

Saadia, tired and frightened, had lain down near her master. He leaned over her and with a kiss calmed her fears. Over four nights they travelled, eating dates and bread. During the day, fearing the *deiras* and *spahis* from El Oued, they kept hidden in the dunes.

Finally, towards dawn of the fifth day, they saw a distant outline of grey walls and low domes. It was the town of Taibeth-Gueblia.

Hama Srir led Saadia into his kinsmen's house and told them, 'This is my wife. Protect her and love her no less than your daughter Fathma Zohra.'

When they were united before the tribal assembly, Hama Srir said to Saadia, 'For God to bless our marriage, your father must pardon us. Otherwise he, as well as your mother and grandmother who did so much for me, might die with their hearts closed to us. I will bring you into your own land, to your aunt Oum-el-Aaz. As for me, I know what I have to do.'

Next day at dawn, he put Saadia, properly veiled, on the family's she-mule, and they descended towards the Rir. They went through Mezgarine-Kedina, avoiding Touggourt, and were soon back in the humid gardens of Remirma.

Oum-el-Aaz was old, and known as a wise woman and healer. She was venerated and even feared by certain men amongst the superstitious Rouara. Dark-skinned and wrinkled under the gleam of her golden jewellery, she was thin and tall, and draped in long veils of dark red. Her eyes glittered blackly out of their deep shadows of *kohl*. Severe and silent, she listened to Hama Srir, then instructed him to send a letter in his name to Saadia's father.

'Si Abdallah will give his pardon,' she said with strange assurance. 'Otherwise, he will not last long.'

Hama Srir entered the oasis and found a *taleb* who, for a few sous, wrote the letter.

'Praise to God alone! Success and peace to the Elect of God!' the letter began. 'To the venerable one who follows the straight path and does good in the way of God, the very pious, the very trustworthy, father and friend, Si Abdallah bel Hadj Saad, at the *bordj* of Stah-el-Hamraia, in the Souf. Salvation be yours, and God's mercy and His blessings for ever! Be assured that your daughter Saadia is alive and in good health, God be praised – and that her only desire is to find herself with you, and her mother and grandmother, her sister, and her brother Si Mohammed, in some near and blessed hour. I write these lines at the order of your sister-in-law, Lella Oum-el-Aaz bent Makoub Rir'i, in whose house your daughter is staying. I have married Saadia according to God's law and I implore your blessing – since all that happens, happens by the will of God. All He requires of us is a ready and gracious response, and to bend our hearts towards goodness. Greetings to you and your family from him who has written this letter, your son and God's poor servant: Hama Srir ben Abderrahman Cherif.'

When this message reached old, unlettered Abdallah, he brought it to Guemar, to the *zawiya* of Sidi Abd-el-Kader. A *mokkadem* read him the letter, then, seeing Abdallah's perplexity said, 'He who is beside a fountain doesn't leave without drinking. Our *cheikh* is here and you don't know what to do. Go to him for advice.'

So Abdallah consulted the *cheikh* who said, 'You are old. From one day to the next God could call you to Him, for no one knows the hour of life's ending. It's much better to bequeath a prosperous garden than a pile of ruins.'

Then, obedient to Djilani's descendant and earthly representative, Si Abdallah submitted to his counsel and requested the *mokkadem* to compose a letter of pardon to the kidnapper.

'... And we inform you by this letter that we have pardoned our daughter Saadia! God grant her His favour, and we call for the Lord's blessing on her for ever. *Amin!* And greetings to you from the poor, weak servant of God, Abdallah bel Hadj.'

The letter was sent.

* * *

Oum-el-Aaz, silent and severe, spoke little to Saadia. She spent her time making up potions and divining the future by strange means, using shoulder-blades of sheep killed at the spring festival, coffee dregs, pebbles, and entrails of freshly bled animals.

'Abdallah forgives,' she said to Hama Srir after consulting her pebbles, 'but he will not last long; his hour is near.'

Saadia became pensive. One day she told her husband: 'Take me to the Souf. I must see my father again before he dies.'

'Wait for his answer.'

The letter arrived. Hama Srir again mounted Saadia on the mule and they took the north-eastern road, crossing the arid Merouan plain.

At the Stah-el-Hamraia fortress a full reception was held, and a great feast, and the affair was never discussed, as there was no more need for explanations. On the fifth day, Hama Srir led his wife back to Remirma. The following month, a letter from the fortress informed Oum-el-Aaz that her brother-in-law had gone on to the mercy of God.

* * *

'Every month I go down to Remirma to see my wife,' said Hama Srir, concluding his story. 'God has not given us any children.'

For a moment he was thoughtfully silent, then, in a lower voice he added, a little fearfully, 'Perhaps it's because we began unlawfully. Oum-el-Aaz says so.... She should know.'

It was very late by now, and the autumn constellations were dipping below the horizon. A great, solemn silence reigned over the desert. We lay rolled in our *burnouses* beside the smouldering fire, dreaming: he, the nomad whose fervent, yearning soul was divided between the joy of his triumphant passion and his fear of the future, the fear of shadows; and I, the solitary, lulled by the nomad's idyll. And I pondered the all-powerful love that guides every soul across the mysterious landscape of destiny.

Bou-Saâda

From the vulgarity of Algiers, its noise and crowds, I fled towards the south, land of blessed silence, wanting to relive, if only for an instant, its life of freedom, far from the hostile atmosphere of 'civilization's' big, foul cities.

So, quickly, almost furtively, I headed for Bou-Saâda, which drowses on the banks of its tranquil wadi, amongst the verdure of its gardens.

I experienced a rapid succession of visions, as if veils were swiftly raised and just as quickly lowered again, on quite dissimilar portions of the country.

First, under a sky blackened by sirocco, the silhouette of Bordj-bou-Arreridj with its old reddish citadel, a small town eclipsed by the immensity of a plain denuded now by the reapers.

In a shop swarming with flies, on a scorching bench, I rest for less than an hour. The shopkeeper is a Sufi of the Zegoum tribe. Grieving, each for our own reasons, we talk about the shining country far away under the marvellous sun.

Then abruptly it's time to set off again in a tottering cart thrown together from boards, harnessed to two starving nags and driven by someone named Bou-Guettar, who looks more like a robber than a coachman.

The heat is overwhelming; a swarm of flies pursues us; the vehicle is having fits. But it's still better than the postal coach.

My travelling companion and guide is Si Abou Bekr, a man of about forty, thin and none too healthy looking, with a tanned, ascetic face and a sad, inscrutable gaze, almost sombre. This man, appointed by the renowned *maraboute* of Bou-Saâda to oversee enormous wealth, wears a very white *gandoura* and *burnous*, but they are threadbare and very simple. Though he lives like a poor man, his spirit is one of great serenity.

Seated together at the back of the cart, our feet dangling over the edge, we speak casually about the south, touching on faith and Islamic jurisprudence.

Si Abou Bekr knows exactly who I am, he's acquainted with my background, and after questioning me closely he expresses approval of my way of life.

In the meantime, I can't contain my joy at seeing the sky clear and the countryside change the farther south we go, becoming harsher and wilder. We pass occasional hamlets built of earth, perched on the sides of dry hills. Midway, on the edge of the *oued* M'sila, we stop to change horses. The square fortress of Medjez with its tall carriage gateway, overlooking the river that winds through a maze of laurel and rose, gives to this relay station the false air of a Saharan caravanserai.

With my complexion I look like a Kabyle, and one of the inhabitants of Medjez insists on speaking to me in that language, assuring me that he has seen me at Tizi-Ouzon, a place I've never been to. I let him talk while we wait to leave. In my new-found gaiety I'm able to laugh at incidents like this.

Back on the road we try to sleep, I perched on a case, and Si Abou Bekr rolled up at the bottom of the cart.

Tenuous sleep, constantly disturbed; half-formed dreams mix weirdly with scraps of reality.

Finally, before dawn, we arrive at M'sila. On foot, we follow a long alley of mulberry trees, arriving at a large square furrowed by little streams where toads sing. At the back there are some ramshackle mud-houses, and in front of a large Moorish café some locals are asleep on mats, their own houses being too hot.

After exchanging greetings with some people I don't know and who, in my half-sleep, seem like mere phantoms, we too stretch out on a clean mat.

I hear, as from a great distance, the commanding voice of a man who is however quite near, on the threshold of the café, waking the sleepers with 'Prayer is better than sleep!' White forms stir, stretch and rise. There's the ring of tin hitting the edges of the fountains. Then everything darkens into the nothingness of overwhelming sleep.

*   *   *

Once again we draw near the wadi, its two banks planted with gardens of a uniform, almost unbelievable green, it's so cool and refreshing to look at.

A few mud-houses stand on a level area: another retreat for Islamic *tolba* who, like the gardens, are dependent upon the *zawiya* of El Hamel.

El Hamel, poetically named, means 'Mislaid', which suits very well this wild and grandiose place, for its seems lost indeed in a valley closed up on one side, and on the other, towards the wadi, open to a vast blue horizon.

The *zawiya* appears to us on the height: two large main buildings, one very white and European looking, the other of pale *toub*, with infrequent, narrow openings.

Lower down there's a settlement of earthen houses, then the village of the Chorfa tribe: a picturesque pile, run-down looking like all clay buildings.

Lower still, a sea of verdure that rises above the date palms like a gorgeous canopy.

The entire sight is crystal clear in the pure mountain air, outlined delicately against the undefinable colours of the hill. This place has a particular look all its own, belonging neither to the Sahara nor to the ordinary countryside of the high plateaux.

In a small room, part of Si Abou Bekr's poor, simple lodgings, I fall asleep quickly on a rug while a joyful coming and going bids us welcome.

Upon waking, I rediscover the calm, reticent, polite conversations which pass long hours of the day. They are typical wherever the great Islamic indifference remains intact, undisturbed by destructive European influences.

Here, in this lost, mislaid place, both grandiose and simple, the noises of our tenacious, useless struggles come to die in the great, immutable silence; and current affairs, noticeably repetitive, become merely incidental.

In order to live with these retiring and sensitive men, one has to penetrate their ideas, to make them one's own, purify them and trace them back to their ancient source. Then life is easy and tranquil in this world of *burnous* and turban, which is closed for ever to tourists, however attentive and intelligent they may be.

Talk little, listen much, do not indulge yourself: these are the rules to follow in order to be accepted and at ease among Arabs of the south.

After crossing several vestibules and vast, dark courtyards, we enter a large interior court, enclosed by very high, old walls of brownish *toub*. In the middle grows a young fig tree which in a few more years will provide shade for this wonderfully silent place. In this court is a sort of bed, a great polished slab placed on four stone supports, where the remains of the deceased *marabout*,

Sidi Mohammed Bel-kassem, are contained.

In a corner there's a woman wearing the simple, white Bou-Saâda costume, and seated on the stone steps leading up to the inner apartments. Her face is bronzed by the sun (for she travels much through the region) and wrinkled. Her age is close to fifty. In the black pupils of her gentle eyes the flame of intelligence burns, but as if from behind a veil of deep sadness. Everything about her – her voice, her manners and the welcome she extends to pilgrims – denotes the greatest simplicity. This is Lella Zeyneb, daughter and heir of Sidi Mohammed Bel-kassem.

The *marabout* had no male descendants, and as successor named his only child, whom he had instructed in Arabic along with the best scholars. He prepared for his daughter a completely different role from the one that generally belongs to Arab women, and today it is she who directs the *zawiya* and its religious brotherhood.

Zawiyas are not, as described by certain authors who know them only by name, 'schools of fanaticism'. Aside from Islamic instruction, *zawiyas* also dispense charity, assisting thousands of poor, orphans, widows and cripples who without the *zawiya* would be homeless and helpless. More than any other, Lella Zeyneb's *zawiya* is a refuge for the outcasts who converge on it from all directions.

Lella Zeyneb, suffering from a painful throat ailment, still struggles courageously against all the enemies who stir up jealousies against her, and never flags in her work of devotion and self-denial.

My circumstances, my way of life and my history are of great interest to the *maraboute*. After listening to it all, she approves of me and assures me of her friendship. But almost at once her smile fades, and I see tears in her eyes.

'My daughter, I have given my life to doing good works, to following the path of God. And men don't acknowledge the good I do them. Many hate me and envy me.

What's more, I have renounced everything: I never married, I have no family, no joy....'

I sympathize with her pain, so undeserved; and hidden till now, only coming to light in the presence of another woman whose own destiny is out of the ordinary.

A rasping cough shakes Lella Zeyneb's chest from time to time. I suspect she is quite ill – and she with responsibility for such a large family of indigents pressing round her. What will become of the benevolent *zawiya* the day, which cannot be far off, of Lella Zeyneb's death?

This female personage, living celibately and playing a major religious role, is perhaps unique in the Muslim west, and certainly merits closer study than I have been able to make during so brief a stay at the *zawiya*.

I spend the night alone, in a vast, vaulted apartment. The mountain wind rattles the window-panes violently, weeps and groans in the valley and among the tombs in the nearby cemetery.

A voice in a dream, melancholy and gentle, wakes me in the small hours. 'God is unique and caring. He has no beginning or end. God is without equal!' the voice sings, ever so slowly.

I get up, recalling sadly that this is my last day here, and go to the window. Below, an old man is strolling, chanting verses of the holy book to an old, traditional air.

I have said goodbye to Lella Zeyneb and left the *zawiya* of El Hamel.

At Bou-Saâda I climb into another crude wagon, packed with Jews and bound for Aumal, across 130 kilometres of jolts and ruts.

Again the zone of red-brown sands, scattered tamarisks, a vast, empty horizon evoking the Sahara I am leaving behind me one more time.

Our first stopping-places have that familiar and well-loved look: of crumbling fortresses, palm trees clustered on low-lying ground. Then everything changes as we climb back towards the high plateaux, the landscape becoming tamed and sad, with a sadness I don't like. It's over....

This seven-day interlude has gone the way of so many others, with me asking myself if it really happened, or if all the fleeting enchantment was only a dream: Bou-Saâda and its *zawiya*, the *maraboute* in white – was it all just concocted by my homesick imagination?

How I was to miss Bou-Saâda... for soon after I departed for boring Ténès, where I lived long months among highland farmers. There I had a good look at relations between the natives and the colonists, concluding that the Arab peasant has the same patience as a Russian serf; while the colonist is usually a good sort, but with no understanding of his neighbour.

From there I often went to Algiers where I would write. One rainy day I encountered Abou Bekr under the arcades. 'You never come south to see us any more. The trees are beginning to flower... the *maraboute* speaks of you often....'

Two days later I was once more *en route* for Bou-Saâda, light-hearted and joyful despite the cold season, as if going to pick flowers from a garden.

July 1902

Homesickness

All the poignancy of life comes, I think, from the absolute certainty of death. If things had to endure, they would seem unworthy of affection.

The sky contains nuances of life's stages: the Past is pink, the Present grey, the Future blue. Beyond this trembling blue yawns the limitless, nameless gulf, the gulf of transformation into eternal life. Yes, the idea of their impending departure, forced and unquestionable, is enough to grant certain beings a harrowing attraction to the things of life.

The places where one has loved and suffered, where one has thought and dreamed, above all the countries departed without hope of ever seeing them again, appear more beautiful in memory than they do in reality.

In space and time, Homesickness is the great enchanter that animates all phantoms.

* * *

And so, he whose soul was elect, during his far-off and successive exiles, needed only an Arab-sounding word, an oriental melody, a perfume, even a simple bell ringing behind the wall of some barracks or other, to evoke with piercing clarity verging on pain a whole world of memories of the land of Africa, dormant, almost extinct, buried in the silent necropolis of his soul; like a funereal, useless mummy inside a sarcophagus that suddenly, at the touch of some secret potion, would sit up and smile like the Priestess of Carthage.

Each hour of his life was dear to him only for this anguish wrought by past and imminent annihilations. Setting foot for the first time on a strange land, he anticipated all the feelings, all the sensations that would be played out in this theatre, and especially that of sadness for his eventual departure, and of the nostalgia to come.

The fact was that he never fixed the contour of things, the form of beings in the present, in the visible realm. He loved to draw them out, to colour them. His imagination was connected with his heart.

Seated on an empty barrel, among the jumble of cargoes on the Quai Joliette, he contemplated the dawning splendour of the pale winter sun, and was reminded of an autumn morning long ago, prior to the great annihilations that had made of him a nomad and a wanderer.

It was at Bône, on the Barbary coast he adored for having left it so many times, and which he no longer dared hope to regain. He had left very early to get to the station, and was skirting the sea, in a suburban countryside so vast and melancholy. Behind Cape Rosa the sun was rising, flooding all the beautiful bay with red and golden beams. The tall eucalyptus trees, browned by the autumn winds, swayed gently in the morning breeze. Some red-breasted birds awoke and sang, hesitantly.

That morning reminded him in the depths of his being of sunrises he'd seen in adolescence and earliest childhood – years of precocious sensitivity and dreaminess, years he had not quite understood except at a distance.

Now, on the quay of Marseilles, in the shadow of the great cathedral that shed on him not the slightest balm of hope, this daybreak, too, was less beautiful than on another day. He saw himself again, elsewhere:

Mounted on his Saharan horse, going along at a walk far ahead of his guides, he climbed a bare hill in the immense emptiness of the African desert. Behind him, the sharp and inhospitable wastes of the Rir valley; before him, a tangle of low walls built of reddish earth, and the shady, delicate date trees of the El Moggar oasis where he would have to pass the day, following a whole night's march. To his left, above the lake bed dried by the summer's furnace, the sun was rising.

The salt plain extended as far as he could see: a solid and reliable route during the summer, traversed continuously by long trains of camels, the gallop of swift Chaamba dromedaries; but a hell of mud and mire from the time of the first winter rains – a murderous route for the fools who dare explore it.

'The great *chott* drank him,' a Chaambi guide said to him, speaking of his own brother. And with a shiver of dread he recalled this sentence spoken on a dismal night of storm and distress, in the very middle of the cursed wilderness, the great Melghir *chott*, treacherous and homicidal.

But that morning, a peaceful sun rose above the plain from which God's blessing must have been withheld since its distant origins, for it bore no sign of life; nothing but the mysterious mineral growths of crystals.

What radiant, smiling peace!

Against the flat, reddish grey *chott*, only the milky flowerings of crystallized salt were to be seen, sad growths that gave off a sharp and nauseating marine odour, emanations of fever and of death.

Yet the *chott*, enemy of life, smiled more innocently than any dawn. . . .

Homesickness! Marseilles was full of scattered reminders, unsettled as huge birds that alight for a moment, collecting themselves before taking off again.

Another time, one melancholy evening, the rain battered furiously on the panes of his window. He had remained alone all day without leaving his room, haunted by a vision from the past.

Around him, the swelling immensity of dunes in the Oued-Souf, like the backs of monstrous beasts, beige faded by excessive light, strange ocean frozen mid-tempest, solidified – only its surface, partner to the winds, flowed ceaselessly in the silence of unchanging centuries. Here and there a shallow valley where, on the pure white sand, bushes of an elfin delicacy, stunted, as if cringing, shed a strange gleaning of dead boughs, black as ebony. Then, at long intervals, milestones along this shifting road through the Souf: The grey *g'mira*, small pyramids of stones built on the crest of the high dunes, marking the route. In the cloudless sky's boundless blue, the evening sun descended towards the horizon. The grey houses and dark date palms of Ksar-Kouinine were lit up against a pink stretch of sand.

With a sudden burst of effort, a panting gallop, his horse reached the summit of the high dune separating Kouinine from El Oued.

From there his dazzled eyes beheld an unforgettable spectacle, a vision of the ancient, fabled Orient.

At the middle of an immense plain, of white verging on mauve, a large white town rose from the shady verdure of its gardens. And this immaculate town, in the heart of this achromatic plain, seemed fragile and translucent against the confluence of earth and sky. With not a single grey roof, not one smoky chimney, El Oued appeared to him for the first time: an enchanted city, as from the vanished centuries of earliest Islam; like a milky pearl, enshrined in a satiny casket nacreous as the pearl itself, which was the desert.

He had no words to express the intoxicating splendour of this sight – intoxicating because ephemeral and of an essential, boundless melancholy.

Tentatively he approached, skirting an indeterminate stretch of small grey stones, tumbledown and aslant in the sand, marking the place of eternal repose for Believers.

And it was there that, into the huge silence of this seemingly dead and deserted city, voices descended as from a mountain's height, pensive and solemn voices which, at the same instant, on the same air of other-worldly sadness, resounded from the borders of Sudan to the Pacific shores, across so many continents and seas, to recall an immortal memory sacred to men so diverse and dissimilar.

But a slower, more measured song rose from a twisting, sandy street. There a long procession of men in white or black *burnous*, some with the red cloaks of *spahis*, emerged quietly, reserved and sad, from the town's enclosure. First came the distinguished elders, whose grey turbanned heads never entertained a thought of doubt or revolt against the divine will. Then, carried on the robust shoulders of six *Souafas*, tanned nearly black, something long on a stretcher veiled in white, motionless in the cold rigidity of death. After that, a line of figures in white and black.

From the group of old men a slow hymn arose, proclaiming ineluctable Destiny, the vanity of ephemeral worldly goods, and the excellence of death, for being our triumphal entry into Eternity.

'Here, Lord, is your servant, son of your servants, who this day has quit the face of the earth. He is leaving those who loved him, and goes to the darkness of the tomb.

He bore witness to you the one God, and to Mohammed your messenger. And you are the Dispenser of pardon and mercy....'

In the funeral valley, two men dug a deep pit in the dry sand. And when the body was lowered into the earth, facing towards holy Mecca, then covered and planted with green palm trees, the white sand flowed softly, reclaiming for eternity the flesh that had clothed a Muslim soul, the soul of some humble Sufi farmer, a man of little knowledge and much faith.

Then, calmly, taking up the empty stretcher, the lines of men headed back up the path towards town, each in the fully resigned expectation of returning at the hour set by *mektoub*, on the same stretcher, accompanied by the same ceremonies and the same litanies of unshakeable faith.

The ineffable gentleness of the burial procession – unmarred by any gloom and doom – set a feeling of profound peace on the stranger's heart.

Other shades, draped in dark blue, advanced towards a well, from whose primitive armature – a palm trunk attached to a beam supported by two posts – hung an *oumara*: a large leather bucket weighted with a stone. These were the women of El Oued going for water, bearing amphoras on their right shoulders, in the age-old style.

On the mud-brick wall of a Sufi house, a complex and chaotic stack of small terraces and vaults, a young man sat down and began playing a small reed flute with magical keyholes. Oh, and then the full impact of his arrival struck him with a pang of sweet sadness he would never forget.

* * *

A freezing squall rattled the sash and panes of his window in Marseilles. He started, as if torn from a dream. Cold, dark night had descended on the town, where he now felt more alone, more foreign. He lit a lamp, intending to work.

His eye fell by chance on to the page of a newspaper where a shipping timetable was printed. A wrenching desire seized him to depart, to relive his dream of a summer's youthful freedom. But after a moment's reflection, he shook it off.

What's the use? The past and its charms are gone for ever. Why should I chase the chimera of dead feelings in places once loved? No! There must be new joys, new sadnesses, new yearnings, in another land.

The next day he left in a fever, eager for sights and sensations. He set off for a different region of the same Africa which held him in thrall, which would be the death of him.

And the homesick wanderer never returned.

Reminiscences

As the stars over El Oued still flicker in my mind's eye, still tremble in my heart, so too do the vaporous, promising beams of the signal lights on the ship that carried me towards the African continent.

Over the course of a few weeks I have discovered the life of Marseilles. I had passed through this great city of departures many times, but always on my way towards a different destination. So I was prevented from exploring it in my usual way – wandering dreamily and alone along the walls and quays and squares, wearing borrowed costumes chosen to suit the place and circumstance.
Dressed as a young European woman I would never have seen anything; the world would have been closed to me, for external life seems to have been made for man and not for woman. Whereas I love to plunge into the pool of common life, to feel the waves of humanity flow around me, to soak up the juice of a crowd. Only in this way can I possess a town and know it in ways the tourist will never understand, despite all his guides' explanations.
But in Marseilles I have always had to run feverishly

through teeming streets, my mind elsewhere, busy with annoying trifles; then, immediately, leaving Marseilles unexplored, shrugged off like a fleeting dream, I would embark for other ports, other countries: to seek silence and forgetfulness in the dormant cities of Barbary; to pursue the mocking vision of a face in Italy's perfect towns; or to stagnate in strange Sardinia.

This time, fortunately, I returned unencumbered, my soul almost at peace, my mind nearly idle, and I have finally managed to penetrate Marseilles, to gather up its sensations, the peculiar excitement of its exotic mélange: the odours of tar, sea-water and orange.

In July 1900 I left again for Algeria. I see myself again at sea... its spaciousness corresponding to that of the desert which fills me with rapture on these first evenings, when the Sahara is mine once more: in this way I live again, at a distance, in what I was yesterday.

The summer sun is slowly disappearing into the open sea, into its tranquil waters. The white rocks have turned pink, and the watchful Virgin on her arid hill shines suddenly with an almost supernatural brilliance.

Marseilles, the city of farewells, is incomparable on these evenings drowned in golden liquor. In the shimmering water fiery serpents run, fugitive and gliding, a warm wind gently caresses houses, ships and water, while on the horizon in the wavering blaze of high sea is enacted the drama of the shipwreck of the sun.

The rusty creak of capstans and anchors raises my heavy spirits; the ship's flanks have shuddered.... It's my turn, now, to lean over the rails and dream, in resigned melancholy, of the unfathomable mystery of days and endings to come, of the fleeting things which encompass and govern our destinies. As certain souls become more attached to their native soil by means of exile, with a love as strong as their hope of return is slight, just so did I begin to love this last town of Europe, especially its ports – and so its dear silhouette burns itself into my vagrant and lonely visions.

But there on the horizon the sea is darkening. The sun has disappeared, and the fireworks are extinguished in purple clouds. White horses appear and run along the dark crest of furrowed waves; long undulations begin to disturb the calm surface of the sea: bad weather is coming.

The ship is away. Marseilles has disappeared over the horizon, with its rocks and white islands – roll on, old ship, transport me!

I've never forgotten this remark by a sailor, told in resigned and laconic tones: 'At sea, there's nothing but fools and paupers.' Certainly the paupers he referred to are the actual sailors, submitting to constant danger and the hardest of lives. As for the 'fools', they are the visionaries and vagrants, the unicorn hunters, those who, like us, 'stand the hazard of the die' – emigrants and aspirants.

Beyond every sea lies a continent; at the end of each voyage lies a port, or a shipwreck.

Unnoticeably, gently, hope leads to the grave. But who cares! Tomorrow will see another dawn, the sea will put on its most shimmering colours, and the ports will brightly beckon for ever.

Memories of El Oued

El Oued: a completely Arab town, situated on the slope of a high sand-dune, with plaster houses built by the Souf dwellers. Its perfect whiteness is what makes it look so Eastern.

The French buildings stand out distinctly; *bureau arabe*, barracks, post office, school, custom-house.

El Oued has two *caidats*, one for the Acheche tribe and another for the Messaaba.

The important Muslim buildings are the *cadi*'s *mahakma*, the five mosques, and the Sidi Abd-el-Kader *zawiya*.

The streets of El Oued are tortuous and all are unpaved. The market is a large square containing two vaulted, domed buildings, one for grain and the other for meat. On market day one sees Souf dwellers of all tribes: Chaamba, and even Tuareg and Sudanese. El Oued's market is held on Friday, and from Thursday evening the surrounding roads are packed with camels, donkeys and pedestrians.

The principal roads are: to the north, the one from Djerid in Tunisia via Behima and Debila; to the northwest, the one from Biskra by way of Guemar; to the west, that from Touggourt via Kouinine, and another via Taibeth-Gueblia, which also leads the way to Ouargla through the desert; to the south there is the road from Berressof and from Ghadames through Amiche; and, to the east, the Tunisian road via the village of Trefaoui.

Around El Oued are numerous villages which make up the region called Oued-Souf.

I have spent months in this land. I came here twice at the height of summer, I spent one winter here, and here I failed to die. Wounded by a sabre blow in the village of Behima, I was here for treatment at the military hospital... but more of that later.

From the first, El Oued was for me a revelation of visual beauty and of deep mystery, the seizure of my errant and restless being by an unsuspected aspect of the earth. I stayed only briefly that first time, but returned the following year in the same season, irresistibly attracted by my memory of it.

I believe there are predestined hours, mysteriously privileged instants, in which certain countries, certain sites reveal their soul to us in a rush of intuition; where we suddenly conceive of them the true, unique and indelible vision.

So, my first sight of El Oued was a complete, definitive revelation of this harsh and splendid land which is the Souf, its strange beauty and its immense sadness. – That was on a hot, calm evening in August 1899.

Fantasia

Of all the extraordinary impressions I have from my sojourn at El Oued – town of a thousand domes, set in an archaic, ageless landscape – the deepest one came from a spectacle I witnessed one clear winter morning, where winters are magical: sunny and limpid as springtime elsewhere.

For many days all the countryside had been celebrating because the revered *marabout*, Sidi Mohammed Lachmi, was due to return from his visit to the distant, almost mythical land of France. This was a rare opportunity to dress up in bright costumes, to race spirited horses through wind and smoke, and above all to let gunpowder have its say.

Day was signalled by a delicate pink glow. Dawn is the choicest hour, most magical of all, in the desert. The air is light and pure, and a fresh breeze murmurs through the foliage of palm trees. No words could render the incomparable enchantment of such moments in the desert's great peacefulness.

We had arrived in time for the vigil at the Ourmes fortress, forty kilometres from El Oued on the Touggourt road, and to meet the holy man there. I spent the night among a small circle of close friends, listening to the *marabout*'s excited, vivid and powerful words. Then I went out to the courtyard where the horses waited, worn out by the unaccustomed noise of the vigil, and by the crowd which had swelled during the night with new arrivals.

Seated or lying on the sand were several hundred men, draped regally in their festive, white *burnouses*. Energetic, masculine heads, bronzed faces set off proudly by the snowy veils falling from their turbans; women in traditional dress of dark blue or red, wearing curious gold jewellery from Sudan, upon which the sun's first beams were flashing like fire.

Around the fires the faithful prepared the humble morning coffee, their attitudes grave, their motions ritualized by nomadic life. Everyone wore at their necks the long chaplet of Kadriya initiates.

Excited by a spirited black mare bred under the burning sky of In-Salah, the stallions were pawing the earth, rearing and whinnying, gracefully bending their powerful necks under their heavy, loose manes.

Outside against the purple sky were silhouetted the strange profiles of three giant *meharas*, placid and indifferent as colossi of another age, disdainful of all this weakling humanity bustling around them.

Finally, at the imperious signal given by one of the *mokkademin*, the courtyard emptied and the doors closed: the hour had come to leave.

The *marabout*, dressed simply in green silk, a green turban and long white veils, as befits the Prophet's descendants, appeared over the gate. Of striking build, serious and deliberate, he halted for an instant and his inscrutable, deep gaze focused on the western horizon. He remained calm and impenetrable amidst the enthusiasm of his followers, his handsome features betraying no emotion.

Amidst the tumult of servants' cries and whinnies of

impatient horses, we quickly mounted. The gates swung outward and in a single furious bound we were outside.

Before us, four negro musicians from the Tunisian district of Nefzawa, wearing brilliantly coloured silks, broke into a strange, savage melody on their strident flutes, accompanied by the thunderous rhythms of an enormous drum.

From the crowd a voice ascended and broke like a wave: 'Greetings to you, son of the Prophet!'

Frantically, the clamour was repeated and tambourines, held at arm's length overhead, beat out a mad rhythm. The startled horses first recoiled, rearing and frothing, then threw themselves forward.

Impassive and silent on his white stallion from Djerid, his eyes lowered, the *marabout* seemed solely concerned with controlling his mount, wordlessly and without a trace of exasperation towards his excited animal.

Finally a sort of cortège formed, white and winding, behind the *marabout*'s tall figure dressed in green.

Slowly we advanced eastward, as if going to meet the rising sun which was still hiding behind the enormous dunes enclosing El Oued.

Our path snaked through blue shadows; then, reaching the heights, our white cortège was suddenly magnified by the red beams of dawn.

The silent, sterile dunes seemed to be spawning crowds of people. Entire tribes descended the hills or surged out of gardens. They formed a large empty circle before us and, with a wild and ululating song, an old war song from days gone by, twelve young men in the brightest Tunisian silks burst into the arena, armed with long inlaid rifles and muskets. Simulating an attack they charged on us with raucous cries, firing their weapons all at once into the sand.

Our maddened horses reared, pawing the air over the

heads of the crowd. Their eyes bulging, mouths scattering froth, they recoiled from the gunfire. But prodded by sharp spurs, they bolted into the crowd which, serpentine and supple, opened a passage for them.

And so at each open, flat place the re-enactment of bravery was repeated. We were transported back to a time when war inflamed souls, drove them, war was joy and splendour. Impulses of ancient heroism and ritual were reawakened in these taciturn nomads, and this procession might have been advancing across the changeless dunes of bygone centuries, for nothing modern intruded on it.

The acrid, dizzying odour of burnt powder clung to us, causing more elation in men and beasts than the savage music and yells.

Before long in the distance we saw, massing on the crest of a high dune, another procession of white robes gleaming gold in the eastern glow. This other crowd advanced, huge and compact, behind three very old banners: green, yellow, and red, embroidered with faded inscriptions and surmounted by shining copper balls. From their ranks came no cries, no shrill tunes; only the clashing of ubiquitous tambourines accompanied a powerful song, rising in unison from a thousand chests.

'Greetings and peace to you, O Prophet of God! Greetings and peace to the holy ones among God's creatures! Greetings to you, Djilali, Emir of the saints, master of Baghdad, whose name shines from the west to the east!'

Near the banners, on a large, flawless mare, rode the *marabout*'s brother, himself a revered *marabout*, Sidi Mohammed Elimam, huge and blond as a Celt or German, his white face brightened by the gentle, pensive look in his large blue eyes – strange eyes under the *burnous* and white turban of Ismail's race, which has been scorched over centuries by the hottest of suns.

The two processions met and joined, and still, from all

the dunes, white spots and blue spots – men and women – poured forth, uncountable.

I turned to look behind us, where a sea of turbans and veils extended out of sight, over the road where I had come so many times seeking silence and solitude. I could see frenetic groups still surging, giving voice to their guns and stampeding the horses.

Over our heads we seemed to be carrying with us a grey, shredded veil, a cloud of smoke.

And the gentle, deep song, sad like all desert songs, billowed and drifted through the pale azure of the sky.

Finally we entered an immense, empty plain scattered with graves. Before us the three *meharas*, which had been joined by others, made their way impassively, steadily, fearlessly through the crowd's midst. Their riders, with faces half veiled, seemed equally detached, perched on their Tuareg saddles. The iron bells worn by the great beasts clanked at each step, and their long heads, thick-lipped and doe-eyed, swayed slowly at the end of their outstretched necks.

But we on horseback, seeing all the open space before us, left the three *marabouts* and elders to march slowly in the shadow of the flapping banners while we took off, finally able to loosen our hold on the reins. There was a furious gallop into the middle of the admiring crowd, then, in the vast plain, circles and curves were ridden at full speed, dizzyingly.

All the repressed madness, combined with the horses' terror finally unleashed, made us fly with abandon. Infected by that impetuous and guileless company, I flung myself into the race with the other riders, forgetting myself.

El Oued, overflowing with more devotees, was passed by; we kept fleeing across the plain and the immense cemeteries, as if a supernatural strength enlivened our horses. Tirelessly, though running with sweat and white with froth, they threw themselves towards the irresistible horizon.

The plain was a multicoloured sea of people, taken over by the ever-increasing crowd, and the three banners now floated above many thousands of Believers.

And the man who was the focus of the throng's love and respect rode on slowly, silently, as if in his own dream.

* * *

Around the *zawiya*'s great domed mosque the plain of El Beyada is deserted and boundless, flooded with subtle blue light.

Out beyond the permanent dwellings an immense nomad encampment rises, a new town of black tents pitched in a day upon the desolate wastes of El Beyada, which are the way to all the mysterious regions of the interior: Ber-es-Sof, Ghadames, black Sudan.

Down there the tambourines' throbbing, rhythmic noise continues; from down there, too, drift songs and other enchanting sounds – the soft and modulated tones of little Bedouin flutes made of reeds.

Up here, a ponderous silence weighs on the decaying mosque, the graves, and the tawny sand.

Below in a small sterile valley scattered with weirdly shaped stones and neglected, anonymous graves, there's a wall, its strangely jagged edge profiled sharply against the night's deep blue. Inside the wall's enclosure, unrelieved by shrub or flower, partaking only of the eternal desert, small stones mark the location of sepulchres. Among them is a little tomb, all milky white, gleaming in the moonlight.

From under the pointed arch of the mosque door a figure looms, tall and dark. Slowly it glides through a space of brightness, then descends towards the burial valley. It enters the walled enclosure and remains there unmoving, head bent in mute contemplation before the small white tomb.

Elsewhere, in the temporary city of black tents, the masses of faithful nomads sing his glory and that of his ancestors, who sowed the seeds of renewed faith across the boundless lands of Islam.

But the tall *marabout*, standing there lost in thought, has come alone into the night to dream; and perhaps to give voice to timeless yearnings, there beside the tomb of his first-born – the son reclaimed by Mystery when his eyes had barely opened upon his resplendent homeland.

Prisoner of Dunes

As I've been ill for some time, suffering intolerable pains in my limbs, with no appetite whatsoever, I've begun to ask myself if I ought to stay here. The idea of leaving doesn't frighten me. I just have no desire to change my way of life.

I've become attached to this country, though it's as desolate and violent as one can imagine. If I were forced to leave this grey 'town of a thousand domes', in its grey wilderness of sterile dunes, I would carry with me for ever an intense homesickness for this lost corner of earth where I have done so much thinking and suffering, and where I have finally found the simple, trusting and deep affection which at the moment is the only ray of light in my life.

I have been here too long, and the country is too devouring, too bare in its menacing monotony, for my attachment to be based on some passing, aesthetic illusion. No, never, I'm sure, has any other place on earth cast such a spell on me, captivated me, as these shifting waste lands, remnant of a great, dried-up ocean, which from the rocky plains of Guemar and the blasted lowlands of the Melriri *chott*, lead to the waterless deserts of Sinaoun and Ghadames.

Often at sunset I lean on the ruined parapet of my eroded terrace, awaiting the moment when the *mueddin* will announce that the sun has disappeared and we may break our fast. Contemplating the dunes – tawny, blood-red, or violet, bleached-looking under the low black sky of winter – I feel a great sadness overcome me, a sort of grudging desperation, as if especially at sunset my mind awakens to the deep isolation of this town. Set behind the insuperable – for so it seems – barrier of the dunes, El Oued is six days from the railway which leads to Europe. And it strikes me then, in the great violet night, that the dunes disguise monstrous beasts that draw nearer and rise up to constrict more tightly the town and my dwelling – last house in the Ouled-Ahmed quarter – in order to enclose us more jealously, and for ever.

Now and then I start mumbling the words of Loti: '*Il aimait son Sénégal, le malheureux!*'

Yes, I love my Sahara, with a dark, mysterious love; deep, inexplicable, yet real and indestructible. It even begins to seem that I could never again live far from these southern lands.

I need to be strong enough to leave, to tear myself out of this confinement.... But I fear that, by my nature, I'm an all too willing captive.

El Oued, 18 January 1901

Marseilles, 16 May 1901
Sensations of evening during Ramadan, at El Oued: leaning on the parapet of my dilapidated terrace, I gazed out at the wavy horizon of the static, desiccated ocean, which from the rocky plains of El M'guebra extends towards the waterless wilderness of Sinaoun and Rhamades. And under the twilit sky, sometimes blood-stained, bruised or blushing, sometimes dark and drowned in sulphurous beams, the great, monotone dunes seem to draw nearer, to gather round the grey town of countless domes, round the peaceful quarter of the Ouled-Ahmed, and round the closed, silent abode of Salah ben Feliba, as if to seize us and, inexplicably, to guard us for ever. Oh, fanatical, scorching land of the Souf! Why haven't you guarded us, who have loved you so, who love you still, whom you ceaselessly haunt with nostalgia and troubling visions?

In the south-east quarter of El Oued, at the end of a blind alley off Ouled-Ahmed street leading to the cemetery of the same name, there was a vast, terraced house, the only one in the town of cupolas. An old, unsteady door of loosened planks guarded the entrance. This door, always closed, signalled the inhabitants' desire to be cloistered from the world and its agitation. The house, already ancient, was built like all Souf dwellings of limestone covered thickly with yellowish grey plaster, and possessed a huge interior court where pale sand from the surrounding desert would constantly turn up.

Salah ben Feliba was the dwelling's original owner, and in this house I passed days which were at first the most tranquil, and finally the strangest, most troubling of my stormy existence.

First there were the quiet times of Chaaban and Ramadan: days spent at humble housework or on excursions to the holy *zawiyas*, riding my poor, faithful Souf; nights of love and absolute security in one another's arms; enchanted dawns, calm and pink, after nights of Ramadan prayers; fiery or pale sunsets, when from my terrace I would watch the sun disappear behind the enormous dunes along the Taibeth-Gueblia road where I became lost one morning....

I used to wait, first for the market's grey dome, then the dazzling white minaret of Sidi Salem, to lose their colour, for the pink glow of sunset to fade on their western faces. At that moment, first from the far-off Ouled-Khelifa mosque, then from the Azezba mosque, the drawling, raucous wail of the *mueddin* called out 'God is great!' and every breathless chest relaxed with a sigh. Immediately the market-place emptied, becoming silent and deserted.

Below in the large open room, seated facing one another, cigarettes in hand, with the wooden case between them serving as a table, Slimane and Abdelkader waited in silence for this instant. And I'd often have fun frustrating them, crying down to them that Sidi Salem was still red. Slimane would curse the nearest *mueddin* for prolonging the fast unfairly. Abdelkader teased me as usual, calling me 'Si

Mahfoudh'. Khelifa and Ali waited with their pipes ready, one packed with *kif* and the other with *ar'ar*, and Tahar poured the soup into a dish, to save time.

And I, fascinated by the incomparable sight of El Oued, watched it turn from purple to pink, then violet, and finally a uniform grey. Thus was my melancholy and my fast prolonged.

Other times, going out at sunset to await my 'redcoat', I'd sit down on the boundary stone near *spahi* Laffati's door. This was at the back of the huge rectangle separating the military quarter and Arab Bureau from the town, and facing the desert that began at the low dune of the limestone kilns, and continued along the cone-shaped dunes bordering the Allenda road. Out there, against the blazing horizon, dark silhouettes appeared on top of the limekiln dune, and as I watched them, profiled there against the purple sky, they grew deformed, became giants....

Then, from the ever-guarded door where the little rifleman in blue was patrolling, bayonet fixed, came the figure in red whose appearance I never beheld without a rush, without a tug at my heart – a pleasant feeling, even sensual, yet strangely sad. Why? I'll never know.

I was seated on that stone one evening soon after dark, when out of the shadows nearby appeared strange little Hania, Dahman's daughter, with her unmistakable laugh – polished and ambiguous – and the voluptuous sadness of her eyes. Wrapped in the dark-blue and red rags worn by Souf women, she was carrying wood to Ahmed ben Salem's house.

The last night I was destined to pass under my own roof was the mad night of 28 January, which was spent in furious love-making. Next day, from the peaceful dwelling of Salah ben Feliba, I departed sadly – knowing I was already exiled, yet still calm – for sinister Behima, whose fatal silhouette has remained graven in my memory just as it appeared to me from the height of the last dunes. At the end of a desolate plain sown with graves, like the one at Tarzant, low grey walls and an immense, solitary palm tree overlooking all. Everything was etched against the sooty grey horizon of that winter afternoon through which the violent sirocco raged, filling the dunes with vapours, stirring up the shifting sand.

At the Military Hospital

For nearly three hours I was tossed about on a litter, crossing the dunes beneath a wintry grey sky, until at last the high vault of the compound gate passed over my head. I noticed the sentinel's impervious tanned face, his sharp bayonet gleaming; then the curious faces of guardsmen; then another, lower vault, a turn to the right – and I was choking on the smell of carbolic acid.

The pain was physical torture, stupid and depressing, against which all one's animal nature revolts and cries; it was fear of being surgically butchered while I lay, overcome and trembling, on the operating-table in the small, bright room.

I can still see this room: its grey wooden door topped by an open transom; on the left, a shelf with a few books, including Drapeau's indispensable almanac. Along the wall, some steaming pans containing pads and bandages, the table of temperatures, the thermometer; then the table loaded with bottles and big enamel basins where barbaric instruments are soaking: pincers, lancets, curettes, scissors, needles, a fully equipped torture chamber... and the bluish spark of the alcohol lamp, ironically flickering like a will-o'-the-wisp. At the back, a high window opens on to the vaulted gallery and the Quartermaster-General's offices. They seem far away in the strange perspective created by the room's uncertain proportions. And here, in the centre, the table where I am laid on a mattress, a black oilcloth under my left side emptying into a pail of bloody water. In front of me, the medicine chest, a cabinet of grey wood. The walls merge into the ceiling's vault, making the room press down like a dungeon or basement. They're the colour of paste, with black skirting-boards trimmed in red. The floor is tiled in grey.

Around me bustle the doctor in his grey coat, with his nice young face and myopic's eyeglasses; Corporal Rivière, his cap pushed back, with his reddish, forked Jesus beard; little Corporal Guillaumin, a beardless youth – all in their shirt-sleeves pushed back over clean white arms, with big bibbed aprons. Finally, in full-dress whites, red belt and regulation *chechiya*: rifleman Ramdane, a young highlander with a calm, open face, a capable man who rarely laughs and is easily nettled by the MO's teasing jokes about religion.

My head muddled, my limbs aching, I'm put back on the stretcher and brought into the next room where I'm laid on a high, narrow bed, unable to settle my bruised body and my horribly painful arm.

At least there's not the torrid heat of summer to perfect the agony. But there's the odour of death, and the nightly visitations by baneful shades, bringing troubled visions, nameless terrors, indefinable anguish, piercing despair – and dictating maddened appeals to liberating Death.

Thoughts of loneliness, abandonment, and dejected sadness, especially since 9 February....

My long, narrow, vaulted room is painted yellow, with grey skirting-boards and a red-brown line of separation, and has grey floor tiles. It's across from the laundry. The signboard on the thick door reads: *Isolation Ward*.

Two beds are separated by the night-table and stool. Over the backs of the beds is a shelf holding a teapot, a tin mug and a white spittoon. On the night-table, a little candle-holder, tobacco, *kif*, and an accumulation of endless, undrunk glasses of coffee.

Across from my bed, fastened to the wall with four paper triangles and drawing-pins, a white sheet titled, plain and simply, 'El Oued Annex – Military Hospital – Rules for Health Service'. This sheet, the work of some sergeant of yesteryear, or perhaps our own Gauguain, concludes with the warning: 'Civilian patients subject to disciplinary measures'.

To the left of the window curtained in army brown: the oil-lamp whose pale rosy light brightens my horrible nights. Beneath it, a military trunk of polished copper.

Sometimes gay, sometimes irritable and acerbic, an observer and thinker, a spiritual seeker, Dr Taste was amazed by me, yet brotherly, admiring and often aggressive – especially on the subject of religion. He very quickly became my friend, an even closer one than Domerg had been – calmer, more down to earth, simpler too. Taste, passionate before all else, often poured out his soul to me, telling me of his mistresses and his ideas, his adventures and dreams. Curious in particular about the sensual world, a seeker of rare sensations, of exotic experiences, he sounded me out on my past, especially the most recent, perceiving accurately that, whatever I might know, the only true and honest knowledge must have been imparted heedlessly by the one person I had truly loved and who had loved me as well; for the miracle of love – one could say the sacrament – is accomplished only when love is shared, and not one-sided.

Taste sought to know Slimène's emotional and sensual characteristics as a way of deducing my own. But he began by completely fooling himself about Slimène, owing to his prejudices about caste, rank and above all race. For the Frenchman imagines the Arab to be instinctive and animalistic, for whom love means the brute act, with nothing to elevate it or refine it. The officer habitually casts the subordinate in the role (and still believes it is too indulgent) of the sentimental musketeer who sprinkles the dubious rosewater of high-flown declarations (in the style of Abdelaziz) over the stench of animal lust. The doctor's interest in these matters, and his sincere admiration for me, increased from the day he saw in Slimène what Slimène even failed to see in himself – the foreignness of his exceptional nature, resembling none other, either for good or ill.

Despite the bitterness of separation from my beloved and the ongoing struggle to defend myself against the prowling wolves, which depressed me and confused me by turns – my time in hospital was one of the most bearable among the recent periods of my life in Africa; I have good and comforting memories of this asylum, this refuge from pain lost in a far-off oasis.

I loved it, and many times since, especially during the dark days at Batna, I missed it. Some called it a military 'death house', the cemetery's vestibule, a corpse factory... all accurate descriptions, too often! But it was also a merciful refuge for the abandoned, exiled, unlucky and poor, for homeless soldiers without family... and this, I believe, is the description that fits it most often.

El Oued, February 1901

After the first days of fever and general distress, and frightful nights – thundering nights without sleep – I'm making a rapid return to life.

Though still weak, I can get up and go out, sit for several hours under the low porch that runs along the south side of the hospital. And there, in an unseasonably hot sun, I experience the good sensation of healing.

But the courtyard is mournfully grey here in the *kasbah* where the hospital stands along with all the other military buildings. This country of rock and sand will never be green. Everything here is changeless, except for the brighter, more golden sunlight that announces the coming of spring.

More sirocco, more grey, heavy clouds. The air is clean and fresh, already the breeze feels warm.

I've grown accustomed to this monotonous, circumscribed life, to the predictable faces coming and going around me.

At dawn, from under the nearby porch of the riflemen's barracks, reveille rings out, harshly at first, like a sleepy voice, then clear and commanding.

Soon after, the big gate creaks and swings open, and

the morning bustle begins. Here in the hospital the attendants rise first, flapping about in their Arab slippers. In a moment one of them knocks on my door, which is merely pushed to; the regulation sheet hanging there on the wall forbids locking oneself in at night. It's Goutorbe, a tall, quiet blond lad, carrying a quart of coffee, and with the same question as every other morning: 'So, Madame, and how are you today?'

It's still difficult for me to get up, and I do it against the good doctor's orders. He shouts a lot and blusters but lets me have my way in the end. My head spins a little, my legs are wobbly, but the light-headedness is pleasant, as if my mind were sublimating itself, the better to receive all the cheerful impressions of my convalescence.

This morning I went to lean over the enclosing wall and looked down on El Oued through the battlements. There are no words to express the bitter sadness of the sight: I could have been viewing any landscape whatsoever, like that of some unknown town seen from the bridge of a ship during a brief port of call. The strong tie which once bound me to El Oued, and to this Souf which I had wanted to adopt as my homeland – this tie was severed painfully, and seemingly for ever. I am nothing but a stranger here.

Most likely I shall leave with the convoy on the 25th, and then my life here will be finished.

I moved away from the battlements to shake off this dismal sadness, and to avoid seeing more of the 'old quarter' and its special, enduring life.

We have here at the moment a rifleman, a tall, thin Kabyle with a bony profile, and sunken, inflamed eyes. The doctor says that this fellow – Omar – is mad. The Arabs say he has become a holy man.

All day he wanders in the courtyard, his head bowed, his chaplet in his hand. He speaks to no one and answers no questions. When by chance during our walks Omar meets me, he takes my hand wordlessly and we walk, hands clasped, slowly over the cloying sand. From time to time he talks to me when we are out of earshot. His ideas are disjointed, but he is not too incoherent. He is very sweet and I've grown used to him.

'Si Mahmoud, it is necessary for us to pray; when you leave here, you must go to a *zawiya* and pray....'

Desert Springtime

Of springtime in the Souf I have seen only snatches, unlooked for here in the 'grey' quarter where, with the barracks, stables and officers' quarters, the hospital is located. In this place all is sand and rock, where nothing will ever bloom.

But the air, at least until the sandstorms came, had grown milder and gentler, spreading a great languor over the countryside during the warm, sunny afternoons when I was allowed to go out on horseback beyond the town.

I also re-encountered the deep Souf gardens, veritable abysses between the sweeping dunes. They were more beautiful than I'd ever seen them, the evening I first went with the MO to take tea at Sidi Lachmi's house. Afterwards we pushed on as far as Elakbab, knowing however that the enormous red-haired *cheikh*, the blue-eyed giant, was in Djerid. So we returned by the garden paths from the east, which leave off at El Beyada, near the dunes.

But where I saw the strange Saharan springtime, in all its sweet melancholy, was on the road through the wilderness, leaving El Oued for Biskra. On this road, after you pass through the fanatical and forbidding town of Guemar, centre of the Tidjanya sect, there's not a hamlet, not an outpost, not a nomad tent, nothing but solitary fortresses with strange-sounding names: Bir-bou-Chahma, Sif-el-Menedi, Stah-el-Hamraia, El Mguebra (the cemetery); and *g'miras*: little stepped pyramids, stone beacons scattered over the stony vastness.

Around seven o'clock I left the friendly shade of the Sidi Mohamed Houssine *zawiya* to join the convoy with which I was to travel: requisitioned camels making the fortnightly provisioning trip for the Arab Bureau. The convoy chief was Sassi, a silent, obstinate man; Lakhdar was a drunken poet who entertained us with his songs; then there were two old men exiled to Chellala; and in addition, a curious band: two pseudo-dervishes, whose profession was begging across Algeria, pretending madness and passing as mutes, who were being sent to Biskra just to get rid of them; an old woman with her son; and some forced labourers, camel-drivers of the Ouled-Ahmed-Acheche tribe.

First, up to Sif-el-Menedi, the uneven plain intersected with dunes and strewn with innumerable dark-green bushes, their red branches twisted, contorted as if in eternal pain; spiny jujube trees; tufts of pale green and gold grasses and silvered *chira* spreading its resinous fragrance through the fresh pink morning air.

At Sif-el-Menedi, a little below the fortress, there's a luxuriant garden walled in clay, like those of the Rir valley. Silvered vaults of date palms; a tangle of fig trees, still without leaves; pomegranate trees and vines covered with pale buds; stalks of fragrant basils and mints. Lower down there are pepper plants, where grasses overhang the murmuring *seguia* with its magnesium-rich water. At night, these limpid streams send up the piping chorus of countless little toads.

Gathered in a corner of the fortress courtyard on a chilly evening, wrapped in *burnouses*, we warm ourselves around the fire. I indulge myself with musings about the strangeness of my life among these remarkable settings. With half-closed eyes I listen to the plaintive songs of the camel-drivers and the patrol. As ever when travelling through the desert, I feel imbued with a great calm. I regret nothing, desire nothing. I am content.

There, for the first time in months, I was seeing earth and fine wild grass, things quite unknown in the Souf.

Farther out, the road descends into the colourful, clayey lowlands which are criss-crossed by dark-brown salt-marshes, now dry; then the road winds round a few peaked knolls of aluminium blue.

From there we enter the region of the great *chotts* or salt plains, one of the strangest places on earth. First we follow a track, slightly gravelly and solid, between treacherous expanses where a thin, apparently dry crust hides unfathomed pits of mud.

To the right and left can be seen two seas of milky blue, stretching towards the horizon, seeming to blend with the pale sky. And beneath the motionless crystal of the salty waters there are countless archipelagos of clays and multicoloured rocks, in perpendicular and stratified ledges.

Not a living soul, not a tree, not a bush, nothing. We notice two small cairns of dry stones, site of an ancient battle to settle a quarrel between two tribes. Their gunpowder had its say; there were deaths....

Some pious Muslim hand must have piled those stones there, to commemorate the dead. Almost thirty years after this obscure episode in nomadic life, the miniature pyramids are still there, perpetuating the memory of dead men, though not their names.

Seen from this elevation, this kind of desert, in the evening after *moghreb*, produces the effect of a swelling sea at the same hour. There's the same dark blue, and the high, sharp horizon. Soon another *bordj* appears, a great grey edifice with a grim aspect, on the crest of a grey dune.

This spot marks the beginning of Bou-Djeloud, a labyrinth of deep canals, islets, pitfalls, of deposits of salt and saltpetre... a leprous region where all the earth's secret chemistries are on display in the bright sun.

To the left, in the west, there's the hazy, imprecise horizon of the Merouan *chott*, now flooded, which extends towards the low oases of the Rir. In the east is the great Melriri, which eventually rejoins the *sebkhas* and *chotts* of Djerid, in Tunisia.

An inchoate sadness hangs over this lonely region 'from which God has withheld his blessing', a vestige, perhaps, of some forgotten Dead Sea, with nothing to boast of but bitter salt, sterile clay, saltpetre and iodine.

Sad ephemeral lakes without fish, birds or boats; sad desert islands, more dismal than a barren dune! For there at least life can be coaxed forth by man, since the soil is fertile. Here, death is complete, and except for the floods of winter, nothing comes to vary the long succession of days.

But despite this they have their splendour and their magic, these valleys of rock salt and transparent lakes where mirages play. Chimeric cities are mirrored there, with forests of palm trees and spectral mosques. Flock after flock come to drink, which are only white vapours distilled by the sun! Land of illusions, reflections, of visions and phantoms, realm of mystery and hallucination: are they memories persisting from the planet's oceanic past? Or symptoms of slow disintegration, leprous omens of the earth's dissolution? Who can tell?

Stah-el-Hamraia, the most imposing of the fortresses, perched on its arid summit, commanding the vastness of the *chotts*, seems a sentinel guarding the wilderness. At the foot of the hill a little, unwalled garden lies flooded, with a few solitary palms, puny, leafless fig trees, and some frail-looking deciduous trees which must be aspens or a sickly species of eucalyptus. Out of the floodwater rise tough, dark grasses, sodden as a drowned woman's hair.

After crossing a reddish zone of clay studded with sharp pebbles, the road enters scrubland. There spring is at its height. It's a riot of green upon green, where everything seems alive and young.

Large Saharan bushes with dark, prickly foliage have been cleansed of winter's dust and clothed in velvet. The shrivelled jujubes, hunched up and evil looking, are covered with round leaflets of an almost golden, tender green; furze bushes are sprinkled with tiny, perfumed slippers; the rushes are plump with sap; tufts of *drinn*, in rigid shining bundles, wave their plumes; here and there an asphodel erects its tall stalk topped by small, pale bells; there are the purple iris and other flowers hiding in the friendly shade of the bushes.

An intoxicating blend of perfumes wafts from all this verdure, these riches poured forth since yesterday for their few days' display until the sky turns leaden and refuses to smile for month after month.

Countless numbers of migratory birds flutter and sing in the festive desert. Larks climb towards the morning light, beating their wings while calling sweetly, then falling again towards the bushes as if in a swoon. But all this fleeting euphoria is overshadowed by the desert's mysterious sadness.

The caravan advances by fits and starts. Camels browse. The men on fatigue duty – tall, brown Souf dwellers of the Ouled-Ahmed-Acheche tribe – hypnotically sing their long, sad laments. Bewildered by all this fecundity, they yearn for their sterile dunes and their grey town of a thousand low domes. The two giant *meharas* stride gravely, bearing their Tuareg saddles and long woollen tassels, their harness bells jangling with every step. The little rifleman,

Rezki, who has served his time and is returning to his native mountains of Djurdjura, sings for himself alone the cantilenas none of us can understand.

Next morning at dawn we leave the fortress of Chegga, built in the middle of a swamp whose saltpetre and iodine are slowly eroding the old walls.

This is no longer the immaculate Oued-Souf, the stark and splendid land of sands. It's unmistakably the salty Oued Rir, a hostile and deadly territory: beautiful in its own way and with its own power to charm.

Since yesterday, when we passed the fortress of El Mguebra, we have been able to make out on the horizon the giant blue scallops of the Aures chain and, below them on the plain, the thin black lines of the last oases: Biskra-Laouta, Beni-Mora, Sidi-Okba.

The approach to Biskra is through a desolate stretch where an actual road is laid out, replacing the charming vagaries of Saharan tracks. No longer a part of the desert, Biskra is no longer the queen of oases. She has been deposed and sullied; her jewels are paste. Now she's a mere figurehead for the crowds to ogle, estranged from the deep and mystic soul of the Sahara.

It is our last evening, unfortunately! We arrive by ourselves at the dusty shade of Old Biskra – and our journey is over. No more long excursions through the landscape of endless sands; no more reveries enjoyed in the shade of holy *zawiyas*; no more chances to wake full of joy in the desert! One last time I turn my horse's head towards the south, and in silence, through the eyes of an exile I watch the darkening Sahara, over which the great red disc of the sun is descending.

Bewitching country, unique land where there is silence and peace across unchanging centuries. Country of dream and mirage, untouched by the sterile tumult of modern Europe.

The sun has disappeared in the distance, and only one red beam lingers on. For a moment, with its sharp, raised edge, its deepening blue undulations, the desert resembles a high, surging sea in the clear twilight.

And since that last evening of spring, I have not set eyes on the marvellous, mournful Sahara.

Oh, the sweet lulling of senses and thoughts by the monotony of life in these lands! The sweet feeling of just being alive, without having to think or act any more, tied down to nothing, no more to regret, no more to desire, except that what is should last indefinitely. Oh, the welcome annihilation of ego in the contemplative life of the desert! Sometimes, however, there are troubled hours when mind and conscience, I don't know why, are roused from their torpor to torture me.

How many times have I felt a stab of regret while remembering my vocation to write and think; my old love of study and books; my intellectual curiosities of old. Hours of remorse, anguish and grief – but these feelings have little effect on my will, which remains sluggish and totally passive. Eventually the surrounding peace and silence take hold of me again and I re-enter the contemplative life, which must be the gentlest, but also the most sterile sort of life. 'You will give birth in pain' was said to the first woman, a decree that propelled the destinies of the first Prometheus of thought, the first Hercules of art. A hidden voice must have said to them: When your mind is released from torture and your heart from its sufferings, when your conscience no longer submits you to the third degree... you will no longer create.

My hand is inert and my lips are still. But I quite understand the universal fatality: it's the delicious and torturing scald of love that makes the bird sing in spring; and immortal masterworks of thought are born of human suffering.

Sojourn in Tunis

During two months in summer 1899 I pursued my vision of the resplendent and brooding East in the old white quarters of Tunis, full of shadow and silence. I lived alone with Khadidja, my elderly Moorish servant, and my black dog, in a vast and very old Turkish house in one of the most secluded corners of Bab-Menara, almost at the top of the hill.

The house was a labyrinth of complicated corridors and rooms situated on different levels, decorated with old-fashioned, multicoloured faience. Plaster delicately carved in lacework bordered the arched wooden ceilings, which were painted and gilded.

There, in the cool darkness, in the silence which only the *mueddins'* melancholy song came to disturb, my days flowed by languidly, sweetly monotonous, and without worry.

The suffocating hours of siesta were spent in my huge room with its green and pink faience. Khadidja, squatting in a corner, fingered the black beads of her rosary, her discoloured lips murmuring rapid prayers. Stretched out on the floor in a leonine pose, his slender muzzle resting on powerful paws, Dédale followed with interest the slow flight of an occasional fly. And I, stretched on my low bed, abandoned myself to the luxury of daydreaming.

It was a time of rest, like a recuperative halt between two eventful and difficult periods of my life. Consequently, the impressions I'm left with from my life there are mild ones – melancholy, and a little faded.

* * *

Between my house and the street were a number of Arab dwellings – inhabited, but behind firmly closed doors. To the rear was a small, old, run-down quarter, a dead end, all in ruins. Panels of walls, vaults, little courtyards, dark rooms, remains of terraces – all were invaded by vines, ivies, and clumps of flowering pellitory and ravenous weeds; a strange district, uninhabited for years. No one seemed to worry about these houses, whose inhabitants must all have been dead or long departed.

However, in the mystic silence of moonlit nights, the nearest of these ruined dwellings came to life strangely. From one of my windows of open grille work, I was able to look down into the little interior court. The outside walls and two rooms of this single-storey house were still intact. In the middle, a fountain with a stone basin all chipped, but still full of clear water coming from I don't know where, was just discernible under the exuberant vegetation that had grown up around it.

There were enormous jasmine bushes spangled with white flowers, tangled with tendrils of vines. Rose bushes strewed the white tiles with crimson petals. In the mild nights, a warm fragrance drifted from this shadowy, forgotten corner.

And every month, when the full moon shone upon the stillness of the ruins, I served as audience, half hidden behind a thin curtain, to a spectacle which soon became familiar to me, to which I looked forward in the days' languor, and which always remained an enigma. But I suppose the mystery is half the charm of this memory. I never knew where he came from or how he entered the small court, but a young Moor clothed in delicately tinted silks and a light, snowy *burnous* came and sat there on a stone, like an apparition.

He was perfectly handsome, with the smooth white complexion of Arab townsmen, along with their almost nonchalant elegance; but his face bore a look of profound sadness.

While he sat there, always in the same place, gazing into the infinite blue of the night, he sang airs of earlier times – graceful cantilenas composed under the sky of Andalusia. Slowly, gently, his voice lifted in the silence like a lament or an incantation.

He seemed above all to prefer this song, the sweetest and saddest of all:

'My soul is seized by grief, as my heart is seized by the night and filled with its loneliness; as the grave seizes a corpse and returns it to dust. For my sadness the only relief could be the sleep of eternal death.... For should my soul reawaken to another life, even to a life in heaven, so too would my sadness be reborn.'

What was the source of this incurable sadness, sung by the handsome stranger? This was never revealed; but his voice, so pure and well modulated, was unequalled in conveying the reticent and indefinable charm of this old Arab music, which had enthralled so many other souls before mine.

Sometimes the young Moor brought along the little murmuring flute of shepherds and of Bedouin camel-drivers, a thin reed which seems to recall in its melodies something of the crystalline whisper of the streams where it grew.

For a long while, in the silence of the late hours when Muslim Tunis was asleep, amid the garden's fragrance, the stranger gave voice to his melancholy longings. Then he went away as he had come, with his phantom ways, noiselessly melting into the shadows of the two small rooms that must have communicated with the other ruins.

Khadidja, an elderly slave, had lived for forty years among the most illustrious families of Tunis and had dandled on her knee many generations of their sons. One evening I called her and showed her the nocturnal musician. She shook her head and remarked, superstitiously: 'I don't know him. . . . And yet I know all the good families of the town.' Then, lowering her voice and trembling, she added: 'God knows if he's even alive. Maybe he's the ghost of a former inhabitant, and maybe this music is a dream, or a spell?'

Being familiar with the character of these people, for whom any curiosity about one's private life or one's comings and goings is an insult, I never dared call out to the stranger, for fear of making him flee his refuge for ever.

One evening, however, I waited in vain. He never returned. But often the memory of his voice and his flute's sweet sighing still grips me, when the moon is full. And sometimes I'm seized by a bewildering anguish at the thought that I'll never know who he was or why he came.

* * *

On the heights, near the vulgarized *kasbah* and the barracks, there is a delightful spot, marked with a peculiarly oriental sadness. It's called Bab-el-Gorjani. Slightly higher than street level, and lying behind an old grey rampart, one first encounters an ancient cemetery. No burials take place there any longer, and the graves are disappearing under a mess of dry leaves shed by rose bushes, in the shade of ancient fig trees and black cypresses.

In Tunisia, access to the mosques and the Koranic cemeteries is forbidden to all but Muslims. As the tombs there are very old and no sightseers pass that way, no one comes to disturb the forgotten dead of Bab-el-Gorjani. Of all the noise of Tunis, only the *mueddins'* calls and the *zouaves'* bugles reach this place, their strains dispersing as they descend towards the motionless mirror of the lake.

Clothed anonymously in Bedouin costume, I have always loved to wander through Muslim cemeteries, where all is peaceful and resigned, and death is not disfigured by gloominess as in the cemeteries of Europe. So every evening I went alone and on foot towards Bab-el-Gorjani.

At the hallowed hour of *moghreb*, when the sun is about to disappear over the horizon, the grey tombs put on the most splendid colours, while the slanting rays of last light are drawn in pink trails over this corner of supreme indifference, of ultimate oblivion.

Farther on one passes under the gate which gives its name to this quarter, to find oneself on a dusty road which, westward, descends into the narrow valley of the Bardo. In the east it leads to the large, maraboutic cemetery of Sidi Bel-Hassene, which overlooks El Bahira lake. This road climbs to the summit of the low hill of Tunis, which is steep and deserted on this slope. I have followed it many times.

* * *

The sun is very low. Mount Zaghouan shimmers in pale tints and seems to immerse itself in the boundless conflagration of the sky. The enormous, flat disc descends slowly, encircled with purplish mists.

Down below in the vast plain the Sel-djoumi *chott* extends, parched by the summer. Its even, lilac-coloured surface is splotched with just a few white, salty crusts, and in this strange light the eye is tricked into perceiving it as a living sea of untold depth.

At the foot of the hill, on the edges of the *chott*, fragrant eucalyptus have been planted to combat the stench of water stagnant with saltpetre. And this arrangement of trees, with their pale, bluish leaves, forms a crown of silver set upon the blasted plain. There I rediscover old impressions from the great Sahara, where the *chotts* are lands of visions.

The last rays of light cast long, blood-red trains on the empty *chott*, on the eucalyptus now completely blue, on the reddish rocks and on the grey rampart. Then, without warning, the light is extinguished, as if the horizon's doors had shut again, and the sight collapses in a bluish mist that creepingly ascends towards the rampart and the town.

It has been said time and again that all the beauty of Africa, so varied and changeable, is the unique result of the stupendous play of light over the land's monotonous surfaces and empty vistas. It was doubtless these effects, these rainbow-coloured sunrises, and evenings of purple and gold, which inspired Arab story-tellers and poets of the past.

* * *

Every day under the gate of Bab-el-Gorjani an old blind man, wearing colourless rags, comes to sit. In the eternal night of his blindness he endlessly repeats his litany of misery, begging alms of the few believers who pass that way, in the name of Sidi Bel-Hassene-Chadli, the great Tunisian *marabout*.

Often, confronting the old mendicants of Islam, blind and decrepit, I have stopped and asked myself if there could still be souls and thoughts behind those emaciated masks, behind the lustreless mirror of their useless eyes. How strange their existence, passed in indifference and mournful silence, so far removed from the men who meanwhile live and move around them!

At nightfall by the gate you may also encounter other ragged creatures, sordid and unnameable: Jews from Hara, or inhabitants of Little Sicily, dangerous and ill-famed districts near the port. They are drawn here by the barracks. Beggars and sometime prostitutes make their way at supper-hour along the walls, and in the dark intersections they wait for the soldiers to venture out. In spite of this, Bab-el-Gorjani remains one of the most deserted and wonderfully peaceful corners of Tunis.

* * *

On a night sadder than most, and feeling inexplicably depressed, I'd been wandering in silent, Arab streets where all activity finishes with the *moghreb* prayer. I ended up at a block of old ruins left standing, by virtue of that grand Islamic indifference, in the midst of streets and markets. It was near the gate of the Souk-el-Hadjemine which by day bustles and swarms with crowds.

There, rising out of the heap of ruins, was a minaret, square and squat – the El Morkad mosque. Except for me, there was no one in the alleys or under the latticed roofs of the *souks*. Tired of drifting aimlessly, I sat down on a stone to wait for dawn.

In Africa, the most delectable of all hours is that of daybreak. The air, still cool and limpid, is so ineffably fine that it penetrates soul and body and intoxicates the senses. It brings a joyous hour of regained youth and reborn hope.

It might have been barely three o'clock and the town was still dark. But below, in the east, the terraces of houses began to stand out blackly on a sea-green background, just barely perceptible.

Above my head I heard the dry clap of a wooden shutter, and a beam of yellow light slid out into the night. The *mueddin* was rising. As if still in a dream, he began his call with the time-honoured assertion of divine omnipotence: 'God is great! *Allahou akbar!*'

Gently, slowly, his voice drifted above the sleeping town. In accents of absolute faith, sincerity and solemn contemplation, this voice came from on high, as if from heaven, steadfast and consoling.

All over town, other voices responded similarly. In a nearby garden birds awoke. And suddenly there was a great concert of vibrant, harmonizing voices, joined in the hymn sung daily throughout all the countries of Islam, to the Lord of the Universe, Sovereign at the Day of Judgement, Master of East and West, King of the dawning day: 'Prayer is better than sleep!'

Like a voice in a dream, growing in strength as it prayed, it sent forth this last phrase on a high, imperious note. Then, with the same dry clap of moments before, the four little pointed windows were closed again. Everything retreated into shadow and silence for the short wait until dawn.

* * *

Smoothly, without haste, the tapering dinghy glides into the cleaner, saltier water of the canal, between the low, reddish banks which lead away from the lake. We head for the open sea, which defines the horizon with a dark line.

We go while the pink of evening still glows, and in the calm, sluggish water of the sleeping lake the dinghy does not even rock.

To the right, on the red and ochre hill scattered with gleaming white tombs and deep-green gardens, stands the bright *marabout* of Sidi Bel-Hassene, and farther off, drowned in mists, the massive old crenellated fort.

The mighty mountain of Bou-Karnine raises its twin peaks, dark blue and already swathed in evening mists.

In the distance, the white cottages of Rhades are reflected in the lively water of the sea.

And here, to the left, profiled against the sky's conflagration, the stately hill which once was Carthage.

I gaze dreamily at this cape, this spur which stretches out into the sea, this corner of earth for which so much blood was spilled.

The white monasteries, remnants of Byzantine Carthage – bastard Carthage of the decadent centuries – disappear in the western brightness. So the Punic hill seems naked and deserted, allowing splendid images of the past to surge forth from the red blaze and reanimate the sad hill: with magistrates' palaces, temples to glowering divinities, barbarian festivals and ceremonies – all that Phoenician civilization, egoistic and fierce, that came from Asia to develop itself and regain its glory on the harsh and burning soil of Africa.

Abruptly the sun disappears on the horizon, and the *mueddins'* solemn voices reach out to me from distant mosques. And the Carthage of my dream, spun from imagination and reflected light, is extinguished on the evening's pyre.

Amira

(From 'An Autumn in the Tunisian Sahel')

During the night a stormy wind drove eddies of rain, drenching the vast plateau of clay where we are camped, with its stripped fields and dense olive groves, intersected here and there by rows of fig trees.

Our poor nomad tents, all sodden with rain, seem so many great cowering beasts, flattened against the red earth.

The sad, lustreless dawn of autumn rises over this changed African countryside, deformed as if by the cold mists that float on the horizon.

Chilled and bad-tempered around a pale, smoky fire, we wait in silence for the coffee that will give us back some of our strength and heat.

It's one of those slow, grey hours when the soul seems to curl up on itself, convinced of the final uselessness of all human effort.

For the past two months, by some vagary of my wanderings, I've been camping among the sullen, untamed tribes of these highlands of Amira which overlook the fertile plains and shady woods of the smiling Sahel.

Having promised a newspaper some travel articles from these parts, I joined up with a small caravan assigned by the Tunisian authorities to make summary investigations and to collect the Arab taxes, which are always in arrears.

The party consists of the little *khalifa* representing the Monastir *caid*: a Moor from Tunis, tiny and thin, very self-effacing – a just man, never cruel and not too greedy; two old Arab lawyers, unmoving in their old-fashioned ideas and attitudes, very gentle, benevolent, smiling. Then Ahmed, sergeant of the *spahis*, an Oranian combining youthful grace, carelessness, sometimes savage violence, and a capacity for reflection much deeper than his rank would seem to demand; finally there are a few Bedouins in red or blue *burnouses*, either *spahis* or *deiras*.

For these two months I've been an onlooker at the activities of these men, whom I never met before I started travelling with them and sharing their life, and who know nothing at all about me. To them I am Si Mahmoud Saadi, the little Turk escaped from a college in France.

And I've hardly opened my notebook, except in remorseful moments when I've managed to scribble a few lines. Once more the Bedouin life, easy, free and lulling, has me in its grasp, making me drunk and drowsy. Write? . . . Why bother?

Into my almost bored musings about my present state, there's a sudden call for us to go down on to the plain to appease a tribe which, to avenge the death of one of its men, is planning a massacre.

We have to abandon everything, entrust the camp to one of the *deiras* who will be busy with matters of transport for this evening, and leave with the *cheikh*'s messenger.

A wild course through the thickets, over soft, slippery ground. We jump ditches, rows of fig trees, on horses unnerved by the wind and rain and who don't want to obey any longer.

But we eventually come to the Hadjedj *douar*; about a

hundred mud huts and low tents on a rounded hill, amid a site of frightful bareness; not one tree or blade of grass.

An unusual excitement reigns in the hamlet, and from far off we hear a terrific noise. Between the tents, men in black or dull-coloured *haiks* whipped by the wind mill about, arguing in groups, obviously angry, while others, squatting, clean and load old flintlock rifles, or sharpen wooden-handled sabres, daggers and sickles. In the middle of the village the women, wrapped in blue or red veils, keen over a black *haik* all sticky with blood, which covers a corpse.

The men are shouting death-threats. As in the times of their ancestral migrations, they are preparing to massacre and pillage the Zerrath-Zarzour tribe, camped to the west beyond a ravine almost a kilometre wide and extremely deep.

The young *cheikh* Ali, magnificent with energy and emotion, comes to meet us, rifle in hand, and explains what has happened:

'This morning, a Zerrath-Zarzour boy named Ali ben Hafidh came here to us with his brother Mohammed, to sell two ewes to my *khodja*. They met one of our men, Hamza ben Barek, from a family they've been on bad terms with for a long time. They were all three up there, on that little rise outside the village. They started quarrelling and Ali ben Hafidh struck Hamza several blows with a *matraque*, breaking his skull. There's his body. The whole tribe and four Melloul shepherds witnessed the crime. But Ali and his brother have hidden in the ravine. Now our people want to go and massacre some Zerrath-Zarzour, for vengeance.'

While the *cheikh* talks to us, the men have gathered round and a great silence falls on the village, broken only by the women's lamentations. Standing with closed, threatening expressions, weapons in their hands, the nomads listen. Barely has the *cheikh* finished his last sentence when the wild clamour breaks out anew.

The gestures and cries are of an unprecedented violence and the angular faces of these lean men become frightening. The *cheikh* Ali throws himself at them again, with exhortations and threats. I hear a tall old man with a beaky profile answer him disdainfully: 'You are young! What do you know? It's the price of blood....' And abruptly the nomads disperse, running towards the ravine.

But the *spahis* and *deiras* also take off in all directions, yelling their own cries. They, nomads in soldiers' uniform, are in their element galloping, shouting, pursuing in mock battle these armed men who at any moment might turn against them and outnumber them dangerously. Every manhunt intoxicates them; their faces shine with the joy of children, boisterous and free.

The tumultuous scene, under the low grey sky, in the furious wind, is savage and magnificent.

Finally the tribe is contained, beaten back to the village and kept under guard. Two or three of the most enraged men are taken and chained. Now it's necessary to begin the investigation, and two *spahis* leave to search for the killer.

He is quite young, this Ali ben Hafidh who is led to us, panting, his clothes in shreds, his face covered in sweat and dirt, his hands tied behind his back. He is pale, but the look in his wide russet eyes is sullen and closed. His brother, a tall, thin Bedouin with the dark face of a highwayman, has the demeanour of a wild animal caught in a trap, ready to spring.... But it's not he who has killed: it is Ali, the little nomad with golden eyes and a beardless face.

In monosyllables Ali ben Hafidh answers the usual questions regarding his identity. Then, 'Why did you kill Hamza ben Barek?' asks the *khalifa*.

The accused seems to collect himself for a desperate defence. He bows his head and looks at the ground.

'Between him and me, God's prophet is witness!'

Henceforth, as in a dream, against all good sense, against all the evidence, he repeats his phrase, his poor phrase of childish denial, scared and stubborn at the same time.

He committed his crime on the bare summit of the hill; there were about a hundred witnesses. With his brother he fled and hid in the ravine. His statements contradict those of his brother, questioned in his absence. But it doesn't matter – to all scoldings, threats, or pleas, he responds in a flat voice, his eyes obstinately fixed on the ground: 'Between him and me, God's prophet is witness!'

For three days we stay at Hadjedj. Three days of discussions, yells, threats, continual alarms.... Finally, when order and peace seem to be re-established, we set off on the trail to Moknine, capital of Amira.

Good weather has returned. It's almost hot, and a fine, tough grass grows all over the red clay made fruitful by the rains.

It's still morning, the limpid hour when the countryside displays itself in azure glory, as if ennobled, under the pink, endlessly pure, pale sky.

Our little caravan advances slowly, despite the efforts of our frisky horses. Accompanying us is a silent, sullen band of twenty-five or thirty prisoners, arrested here and there among the tribes. Resignedly, without a gesture or word of revolt, they march, chained two by two at the wrist and ankle. They seem indifferent to their fate.

Ali, the only murderer, has his arms tied behind his back, his feet hobbled, and walks apart between the *spahis'* horses. He maintains his impenetrable expression, and when the Bedouins of his tribe manage to shout a few words of farewell from a distance, he answers with a firm voice, as if it's the truth: 'Between him and me, God's prophet is witness!'

The Hadjedj tribesmen, now appeased, watch him pass: silently, their hatred diluted, for he is now in the hands of human justice, which nomads instinctively dread and mistrust. Ali himself is no longer the enemy whom they have the right to kill, blood for blood. He is a prisoner, which is to say an object of pity, a victim of that dreaded and hated phantom: Authority. The hatred and vengeance of the Hadjedj people would now sooner be directed at the entire Zerrath-Zarzour tribe than at Ali, if they had a choice.

Suddenly, from a ravine hidden by fig trees, a group of women run out at us, wailing and pleading. The eldest of them, led by a beautiful, black-eyed girl, is blind. Her white hair falls across her wrinkled forehead, and she's weeping.

Still guided by the little girl, the old woman hangs on the *khalifa*'s stirrup, imploring, 'Sidi, Sidi, for the sake of your own mother's soul, have pity on my only son, my Ali! Have pity, Sidi!'

Our convoy has stopped and all our men grow serious. Our hearts are wrung by the suffering of this blind old mother in rags, whom we are powerless to console.

The *khalifa*, on the verge of tears, babbles promises that he'll never be able to keep, and Ali's mother showers blessings on him. Then she turns and falls upon her son's chest, lamenting as over a corpse.

Going pale, the little Bedouin trembles all over.

'Your father is in bed in the hut,' says the old woman, 'and he is ill, very ill. His hour has surely come. He sends a message that if you have committed murder, you should confess, so that God will have mercy on you and on us, and so that the tribunal might be more lenient.'

Then suddenly, convulsively, Ali begins to cry, his young

face becoming like that of a child. In a low voice he murmurs, 'Forgive me, Muslims! I have killed a creature!'

The horsemen and Bedouins who have gathered round exchange these joyous words: 'He has confessed! He has confessed!'

Those words trigger Ali's transformation, for all these people, into an object of deepest pity and concern. The sergeant Ahmed, usually a hard man, leans over Ali and unties his hands. 'Embrace your mother,' he says.

There follow goodbyes interrupted by sobs, cries and the women's laments. Then the disconsolate group draws back, but for a long time we can hear the old mother, tearing at her face and shrieking horribly.

The sergeant allows the Zerrath-Zarzour people to approach Ali, to bid him farewell and give him a few copper coins to help feed him in prison. Among those bringing alms for the prisoner I recognize two or three old men from the Hadjedj tribe, some of the very ones who, only the day before, wanted to massacre Ali and his people.

'Here. Accept this from us, who wish to follow God's path,' they say to him. Then they step back, gravely.

Soon the sergeant has to disperse everyone, for the Zerrath-Zarzour crowd is dense and could prove dangerous. So we start off again along the trail to Moknine, through olive groves, where we shiver among the dewdrops.

September–October 1899

Bled-El-Attar

(The City of Perfumes)

In one of the oldest quarters of Tunis, quite near the holy mosque of the Olive – Djemaa Zitouna – everything expresses serene antiquity and unshakeable faith. This little district of shadow and sensuousness simmers like a conspiracy of pleasures, with the exquisite colours and enticing perfumes of the El Attarine *souk*.

The *souk*'s high vaults rest upon spiralled colonnades painted red and green. Underneath, shady paths intertwine, evocative and full of mystery. To the right and left of the paths, small closet-like perfume shops disclose their waxen-faced Moorish proprietors, whose gaze is softened by the dim light and their senses enfeebled by a surfeit of fragrance.

Among the young merchants was one who was thoughtful and full of natural refinement, named Si Chedli ben Essaheli, son of a pious and learned jurist of the Zitouna mosque.

Si Chedli loved to dress with the discreet elegance of certain Tunisians who know, from long tradition, how to wear silks of subtle colours, their delicate shades borrowed from the past.

Leaning nonchalantly on a precious mother-of-pearl chest, Si Chedli would read old Arab books of stories or poetry.

From the entrance you'd notice a small table before him holding a cup of rosewater coffee and a pipe of *chira*. And from a translucent vase of fine blue porcelain a huge magnolia blossom would greet you, inviting you in with its four thick petals of redolent flesh.

'What are you thinking about, Si Chedli?' was often asked by his friends from the *souk*, with whom he was naturally distant and reticent.

'I am thinking that all human joy is a phantom, and yet this is my greatest distraction....'

* * *

One day a carriage stopped at the entrance to the *souk*. A group of veiled women alighted and entered the shaded arcade with swaying step. Eventually they found themselves at Si Chedli's shop, which caught their eye, resembling as it did a large, carved wooden box.

The young man noticed immediately that they were strangers, for they wore the pointed caps of Constantine women, poised saucily on the side of their heads.

The youngest sat down on the bench and began chattering with the chirping prattle of a bird.

Her long, slim, henna-tinted fingers played for a while with faceted decanters, ivory boxes and aromatic pastilles. After settling on a price she rose and gathered together the things she had chosen. Then, quite nonchalantly, she said, 'Send these to me at the house of Lella Haneni, in the Halfaouine quarter.... No, don't send them with the porter, for these are precious essences ... you must bring them yourself.'

As the Moorish woman left the shop, Si Chedli's eyes met her own insistent gaze. He was shaken, yet failed to turn his head aside before an answering smile escaped him.

'When?'

'This evening, after *moghreb*.'

When the hour came for prayer, Si Chedli went to the mosque as always. But he left discontented, having prayed hastily, his soul troubled and preoccupied.

* * *

The red glow from the west still lit the heights of the town on the Bab-el-Gorjani side; a languid calm was wrapping Tunis in a final mist of colour.

His pace more brisk than usual, Si Chedli set off to Halfaouine through the sluggish crowds in front of the shops.

He entered a vaulted cul-de-sac and paused before a small, incredibly low door. The heavy iron knocker resounded strangely in the decrepit old house, where rank weeds had begun to encroach.

'Who's there?' cried a tremulous old woman's voice.

'Open up!' An Arab never gives his name in the street, even in front of his own house.

The door opened half-way and an old woman appeared, dressed in the blue *fouta* of poor Tunisiennes. 'You come from the El Attarine *souk*?'

'Yes.'

She led him into a large court where three orange trees were planted. On the first-floor gallery, the arched opening of a doorway was veiled with silk, bright as a pomegranate flower.

'She's there. Go up!'

In the cool shade of a stairway paved with blue faience Si Chedli climbed, breathless with anticipation. He parted the soft curtain, which twisted round his hand like a gorgeous flame. There, on a thick rug from Djerid, among cushions embroidered with dull gold, a woman lounged in a chemise of white gauze with wide, spangled sleeves, a green and gold velvet caftan, and several silk *gandouras*.

She still wore, even lying down, her pointed *chechiya* adorned with a fringed scarf and two fine golden chains which joined just under her chin, setting off her smooth face and brightening it.

'You are welcome. Sit down.'

Her beauty was the indefinable sort – of a proud yet radiant quality, subtly betraying a hidden warmth.

He sat beside her, and an old Moorish woman brought the obligatory coffee on a small tray of chased copper.

'Are the women of Tunis as beautiful as Mannoubia?' asked the old one, showing her toothless gums as she laughed.

'Mannoubia? ... She is a rose hidden among leaves.'

'You too are very handsome.'

Mannoubia played distractedly with a fan, her bracelets ringing slightly with each movement. Her precious ankle-rings jingled when she stretched her feline body across the soft wool. She hadn't the boldness of Tunisian courtesans. In front of Mannoubia, Si Chedli could not achieve the manner he would have adopted with another. There was something like fear between them: fear of joining, fear of the struggle for more than mere pleasure.

'Listen,' she said, 'I went to buy perfumes, as a distraction ... but when I saw you, my heart desired you more than the most precious essence. Why don't you say something? Why do you cause me such shame?'

'But who are you? Where do you come from, to disturb my sad tranquillity?'

'Bône is our native town, but I grew up in Constantine, with my aunt, my mother's sister. I came here because I was bored.'

Chedli, brushing against Mannoubia's knees, his eyes reflecting all her allure, murmured, 'No. You have come like the rain to the desert.'

The golden chains trembled against her cheeks.

The old woman had disappeared, leaving the couple in the silence and euphoria of falling night, where they prolonged the sweet agony of their desire.

Mannoubia let her head slowly fall, the loveliness of her neck and the flush of her throat seeking a response against Si Chedli's clamorous heart. He embraced her, their kisses growing in fervour until they fulfilled the promise of Eden.

* * *

From that day, Si Chedli often deserted his shop and neglected his old books. He was living in a dream.

Si Chedli was twenty-five years old and had availed himself of all pleasures to the point of satiety. He had never suspected that love could have enough force to change all aspects of the universe.

It seemed all of nature fêted him when at nightfall he took the path to Halfaouine. During the delicious lassitude of his mornings, when he bathed, it seemed that a thin veil was being torn, letting jasmine petals fall on to the earth. Even on his way to prayers, the air was redolent of his love.

Chedli shared his secret with no one, the better to immerse himself in it; and, seeing him so pale, some people feared he was ill.

But the old, strict Si Mustapha Essaheli, seeing the considerable change taking place in his son, had him discreetly spied upon. Before long the secret of Mannoubia's retreat was known to the old man.

One evening, Si Chedli's knock at the door was answered by the old Tunisienne in tears: 'They have taken your dove!'

'What do you mean?'

'Yes, Sidi. Today some of the Bey's men came, they took her and old Teboura, though she cried out your name and protested.... They took her to the station and put her on a train for Algeria.'

Chedli remained calm and serious; he asked no questions, still finding the story incredible. He entered the white, deserted court, climbed the stairway of blue faience, pulled aside the curtain and saw the empty room. Then his eyes seemed to drain of all life.

'I'll find her again, I swear it by God and Mohammed! I swear it by the blessed *cheikh* Sidi Mustafa-ben-Azzouz, my master in this world and the next... I shall find her.'

* * *

For a long time, patiently, he searched for a trace, a clue. Finally, through some friends, he learned that Mannoubia had returned to Bône, where, so they said, she was living a courtesan's life.

Chedli's heart leaped at this news, leaped with hope more than anger. He would go to his love, would hold her, would erase all the insincere kisses with the sincerity of his tears. They would transform all the suffering and shame by their love. But while his father lived, Si Chedli possessed nothing of his own. He begged the old man for permission to leave, but in vain. Then, abandoning the shop, he haunted the cemeteries and the outlying ruins.

One day he failed to return. His father searched everywhere for him; but Si Chedli was gone, driven by the force of his love.

It was the old man's turn to weep.

* * *

For a long time, in the old alleys, in the Moorish cafés of white Annaba, Si Chedli sought news of Mannoubia. He searched everywhere, both among those who had nothing to do with women, as well as in all the prostitutes' houses.

Eventually it was a year since Mannoubia's disappearance. Bewildered by conflicting information, Si Chedli had become stranded in Algiers.

One evening, at a café in Bab-el-Oued teeming with different races and smelling of anise, Chedli met one of his old friends from Tunis, now a sergeant in the riflemen's detachment. They exchanged reminiscences.

'Mannoubia bent Ahmed El Kharrouby? – I knew her.'

'What's become of her?'

'God grant her peace!'

Chedli was crushed, prostrated. In that instant it was as if a door slammed shut, of a dungeon from which he would never escape. He'd abandoned homeland, family, wealth, to become a vagabond. Having sought his lover for a year, misguided yet ever hopeful... he had come all this way to learn that she was dead!

'But when did she die? Where?'

'At Bône. She returned there about a month ago, after being in Algiers for some time. She was in great pain, but always laughing at everything... she was drinking. In the end she died of consumption.'

'Ali, do you by any chance know how to find her grave there?'

'No. But Teboura's other niece, Haounia, will show it to you. Teboura is also dead.'

* * *

Behind Idou's sullen blue peaks the noble sun descends, embracing the surrounding heights and the sacred hill planted with tall black cypresses and sinuous fig trees.

There Muslims come to sleep the inexplicable sleep of the grave, under gracefully sculpted stones of various colours.

Neither gloomy nor sad – this cemetery full of flowers, vines and bushes, where tombs of faience and white marble are mere spots of purity upon the living earth. Everything here expresses great calm and resignation; an unshakeable, consoling assurance.

From this garden of absolute peace, this edge of a dream, extends the immense, unmoving gulf of opaline pink streaked with azure and gold, its beauty increased by the sky's extravagance. Under their lateen sails, scudding feluccas seem poised in ether between two mirrors of the infinite.

On the sanctified hill, shaded by a young fig tree, is a tomb of blue and white faience, carved with a woman's body lying between two dressed stones. One can read there, in Arab characters, this simple epitaph:

Mannoubia bent Ahmed
from Constantine.
Everything returns to God
There is no other divinity but God
and Mohammed is God's messenger

Sometimes at the seductive hour of *moghreb*, when the immense rose of evening blooms, a man dressed in coarse cloth, with regular, unsmiling features, climbs to the silent necropolis, to await nightfall alone with his dreams.

He wears a blue rifleman's uniform; under his red *chechiya* his face has become tanned and thin, and no one would recognize in this rugged soldier the delicate and pale Moor of Tunis.

* * *

In the El Attarine *souk*'s heavy silence and fragrant shade, in the shadow of the nearby Zitouna mosque, is a shop that resembles a cell. Amid the halo of multicoloured tapers and perfumes an old man sits, his thin arm leaning on a mother-of-pearl casket, as if it contained all his memories. For hours and days he stays there, immersed in his unchanging dream, and he waits – features pinched, branded with pain; his eyes dulled and discoloured by tears.

He stays there and waits, a witness of time, like a mocking statue of himself. He hears the workings of his heart growing slower and fainter. He thinks of his son who will never return, and how little power is left to him, now he is going to die.

Marseilles, May 1901

There are so many miserable people, hopelessly besmirched by their daily grind, who spend life's brief hours in useless, absurd recriminations against everyone and everything. They are blind to the ineffable beauty of things, to the sad splendour of suffering humanity.

Happy is he for whom nothing proceeds bestially and cruelly by chance, to whom all earth's treasures are familiar, for whom all does not end foolishly in the darkness of the grave!

They are deformed beings who view the world through a jaundiced eye, seeing nothing of inexhaustible Beauty, which is the very essence of the Universe and of Life.

The most destitute of all the world's outcasts, an exile without home or country, a dispossessed orphan is she who writes these lines. They are sincere and true.

Often, in carefree times of prosperity, I have found life boring and ugly. But now that I have nothing but my ever-watchful mind, and since my soul has been tempered by suffering, my feelings are completely open to the wonderful mystery that saturates all things.

The Bedouin herdsman, unlettered and unaware, praises

God at sunrise facing splendid desert horizons, and praises Him again in the face of death. He is altogether superior to the pseudo-intellectual, who piles sentence upon sentence just to denigrate a world whose sense he cannot fathom, and to insult Suffering, that beautiful, sublime and benevolent educator of souls.

In the past, when I lacked nothing materially, but lacked everything intellectually and morally, I was often gloomy, endlessly cursing Life while having no real knowledge of it. It is only now, in the midst of a destitution of which I am proud, that I acknowledge life as beautiful and worth living.

Three things can open our eyes to the dazzling promise of truth: Suffering, Faith, and Love – all of love.

Glossary of Arab Terms

alfa: desert grass.
Aman: Assurance; security; protection.
ar'ar: aromatic plant used for smoking.
bendir: nomad's drum.
bordj: fortress; citadel; tower.
burnous: large, woollen, hooded cape worn by men.
cadi: Muslim judge.
caid (pl. *caidats*): leader; commander; during colonization, a local functionary representing France at the head of a tribe.
chechiya: skull-cap, coif or caul.
cheikh: chief of a division named by the governor, subordinate to the *caid* and controlling many *mokkademin*; old man; spiritual director; chief of a brotherhood.
chira: grass; barley.
chott: dry salt lake; enclosed depression in arid regions, the bottom of which is occupied by a *sebkha*.
deira: municipal guard; patrol.
djemaa: local assembly of inhabitants of a *douar*; mosque.
douar: cluster of dwellings most often consisting of families who claim common ancestry; group of tents; village.
drinn: desert grass.
fouta: towel taken to Moorish baths; sometimes worn as a skirt.
gandoura: sleeveless tunic of wool, silk or cotton worn under the *burnous*.

g'mira: landmark or milestone indicating a track.
guerba: water-bottle of goatskin.
haik: large, square white veil; or woman's veil.
hassi: well.
kasbah: originally a citadel or space surrounding the palace; by extension, old Arab town.
khalifa: vice-governor of the Tunis Bey's *caidats*; local functionary attached to the *caid*.
Kharatine: descendant of black slaves from southern territories.
khodja: secretary; interpreter.
kif: hashish.
kohl: eye make-up; powder of antimony.
ksar (pl. *ksour*): Saharan village.
mahakma: local court of justice.
makhzen: auxiliary corps of the police or army, composed of natives, to keep the peace. Also refers to the Moroccan police force.
marabout(e): holy personage; object of popular veneration; location of a sepulchur or holy place.
matraque: Arab bludgeon; big knotted stick.
mehara: racing camel.
mektoub: what is written (in the Koran); destiny; the will of God.
moghreb: where the sun sets; hour of sunset.
mokhazni: *makhzen* cavalry.
mokkadem (pl. *mokkademin*): director of a *zawiya*, appointed by the *cheikh*.
mueddin: person in charge of calling to prayer.
oued: watercourse; valley.
oumara: leather water-bottle.
Kadriya: brotherhood founded in the twelfth century by Abd el-Kader Djilani of Baghdad.
Ramadan: religious fast observed during daylight hours, for the month of Ramadan (ninth month of the Hegira).
sebkha: salt marsh.
seguia: open irrigation canal.
Souf: region of sand-dunes in south-eastern Algeria.
Souafa: inhabitants of the Souf.
souk: Arab market; rural market.
spahi: Algerian native trooper.

taleb (pl. *tolba*): student; literate Muslim; sage.
toub: dried clay.
zawiya: religious establishment; school; seat of a brotherhood centred upon descendants of a local saint.
zouave: soldier in Algerian infantry.